Love Conquers All

ROSEANNE WILLIAMS

Harlequin Books

TORONTO • NEW YORK • LONDON
AMSTERDAM • PARIS • SYDNEY • HAMBURG
STOCKHOLM • ATHENS • TOKYO • MILAN

Published June 1991

ISBN 0-373-25450-4

LOVE CONQUERS ALL

Printed in U.S.A.

Too cl

In the dar a
in his arms, whispering his promise that she had nothing to fear as long as he was with her. There was nothing wild in that promise, but the blood raced through his veins as he made it.

"Ty, I didn't come out here for this . . ." Rianna admitted.

"I wasn't banking on this, either," he murmured against her temple.

"We shouldn't. . . ."

"No," he agreed in a whisper, "we shouldn't. We should go back to our separate bedrooms, but we're not going to, are we?"

"No, we're going to . . . We've been moving toward this all night." It was insane to want to make love to a man her father would hate on sight, Rianna thought. Still, being in Ty's arms seemed sane and logical rather than crazy. Here in the dark, she was simply herself; he simply himself. Nothing complicated about it. "Ty. . ."

Ty knew he'd regret a slew of things in the morning if they made love. But he would regret it more if they didn't. He lowered his head to kiss her, and invited . . . regret.

Roseanne Williams just *loves* animals. Milo, her beloved six-year-old cat, who lives with Roseanne and her husband in California, will certainly attest to that. Roseanne also has a keen interest in wildlife preservation. A TV documentary on the smuggling of endangered species into the States gave Roseanne the idea for *Love Conquers All.* Roseanne says we all should be concerned for we, too, are a species. She is currently working on her next Temptation.

Books by Roseanne Williams

HARLEQUIN TEMPTATION

237–HOW SWEET IT IS!
306–THE MAGIC TOUCH

1

"PLEASE. Don't. No, don't move," Rianna Breece whispered as she backed away from the ten-foot python on the Persian rug.

The snake slithered forward. Rianna froze. It flicked out its forked tongue to the toe of her boot. It tasted the hem of her jeans.

"Stay," she pleaded softly. "Stay still. Right there. Not one inch closer. Please." She took another step back.

Click. Whir.

Gotcha.

She lowered her Nikon camera and let it rewind its roll of thirty-five-millimeter film. "Great close-up, Squeeze-Play," she said to the snake. "I've got enough film on you now to paint more than one full-length portrait if the first one doesn't work out. Squeeze, old girl, you're a perfect ham—for a reptile."

"Ham's one of her favorite snacks." Gordo Davies chuckled and knelt to stroke his pet snake's stomach. "Squeeze can't help it if she *is* what she eats."

"She's not the only one," Rianna said, patting her own middle. "Lately it's been too many Big Macs for me. I can hardly wait for the gourmet dinner I'm having tonight with a handsome hunk I know."

"Really?" Gordo hauled up his lanky frame and scratched his sandy head. "You have a date? Who?"

"Don't look so amazed that I might be having dinner with a man."

"I can't help it. You haven't dated anyone since that scum Brent last year. Who's the lucky guy?"

Rianna smiled. "I'm looking at him. I always take my clients out to dinner before I start painting the exotic pet portraits they commission."

"Me? I'm not a client. I'm only your cousin. So what if my exotic pet's the one you want to practice painting before you paint the snake posters for that zoo? You don't owe me dinner for it."

"You're also," Rianna pointed out, "the man whose fiancée begged me to keep an eye on him while she spends the weekend in San Francisco shopping for her wedding dress."

"That's my Chloe." Gordo grinned. "She's almost as possessive as Squeeze."

"You love every minute of it," Rianna affectionately accused him. "Let's keep Chloe happy—and me, too. I haven't sat across from anything but an empty chair at a good restaurant on a Saturday night since Brent's disappearing act. How does dinner at Casanova sound?"

"Too classy to waste on family. Save Casanova for a bona fide dinner date. It's enough that you're painting Squeeze's portrait for a wedding present."

"How could I do otherwise when she's the one who literally brought you and Chloe together at the pet shop?" Rianna pursed her lips. "As for bona fide, my last date could have posed for a real snake and saved Squeeze the trouble."

"Careful," Gordo warned. "You know how touchy she is about the species."

"The last man I went out with was a real sidewinder and an octopus, too. Wasn't he, Squeeze?"

As if on cue, Squeeze-Play hissed.

"See? Squeeze agrees. You know that son of a friend Aunt Penelope was endlessly raving about? *He* was the sidewinder with eight hands he couldn't keep off me and every other female at the party we went to. So much for Aunt Penelope's rave reviews. Come on, be a sport. Dinner's on me."

"Well, you know I rarely pass up a free meal, but I'd planned to eat pizza and play poker with the boys tonight. I won't be a bachelor much longer, you know."

"I know. And I'm teasing about playing watchdog for Chloe on a Saturday night." Rianna removed the finished roll of film from the camera. "The truth is...I have my own reason for wanting company tonight."

"It better be good."

"It is." She took a deep breath to control the trembling of her fingers as she stored the film in a plastic tube. "I think I'm being followed, Gordo."

"What?" He stared at her for a moment, then placed a hand on hers to still the trembling. "What do you mean 'followed'?"

She bit her lip. "Followed by a man."

"What man? Who?"

"I don't know who he is." Rianna sank onto Gordo's couch and raked a hand through her short blond hair.

Gordo frowned and sat down, too. "How long has he been following you?"

"A few days. At least, I think it's been that long." She thought for a moment. "I'm not really sure. I first noticed him on Wednesday when I drove down to Big Sur to have lunch at Nepenthe with a friend. You know what a great place the terrace is for people watching."

"I know what a super place it was for *girl* watching before I met Chloe. Was he doing the same thing?"

"Not that I was aware of at first. He was there like everybody else, eating a hamburger and drinking a beer. Cybil spotted him and pointed him out."

"Cybil, the gorgeous redhead who tends bar at the pub on Ocean Avenue?"

"Mmm-hmm. We have lunch together every so often."

"So Cybil was boy watching, was she? She never gave me the time of day before I met Chloe."

"That's her loss and Chloe's gain," Rianna said to soothe his ego. "Cybil's so choosy she rarely gives any man the time of day."

"Like someone else I know," he chided. "But back to you being followed. Why did Cybil point this guy out at Nepenthe?"

Rianna sighed. "It's this little matchmaking game she plays. 'This one's my type, that one's yours,' and so it goes. She decided the man in question was definitely my type."

"Nothing like Brent, I hope."

"No. Far from it. Early thirties. Medium height. Black hair. Japanese with classic features. Cybil kept craning around to look at him and marvel to me about what a hunk he was."

"When she craned around more than once, did this hunk take notice?"

"I couldn't tell. Right after she convinced me to turn around and look, he put on a pair of sunglasses. The mirrored kind." Rianna shivered slightly. "I kept feeling his eyes boring into my back during lunch. You know that feeling you get when someone you can't see is staring at you?"

"Yeah. What happened after lunch?"

"Something magical, actually. An April shower blew in from the sea. It never quite reached Nepenthe, but the sun was just at the right angle and a double rainbow appeared. It was . . . beautiful beyond description."

Gordo rolled his eyes. "You and your rainbow fetish."

Rianna rolled her eyes. "You and your snake fetish."

"Touché." Gordo chuckled. "Was your secret admirer bowled over by the rainbow, too?"

"I don't know. *I* was so bowled over I forgot about him. When I turned around to check, he was gone. But I keep seeing him here and there around town—usually out of the corner of my eye. Yesterday at the post office I could have sworn he got into line two people behind me. But when I left the stamp window he was gone. And later, when I went over to the art supply, I saw him looking at easels. When I looked again, though, he'd vanished...."

"He's never approached you or spoken to you?"

"No."

Gordo shook his head. "Hey, it's probably just a coincidence. Carmel always has more than its share of tourists, even in April. He's probably a tourist from Japan on his first trip to California."

"I don't think so, Gordo. He's never carrying a camera, for one thing."

"Even so, what makes you so sure he's following you?"

"I'm not sure of anything." Rianna sat silent for a minute, watching Squeeze glide over the arm of the couch and onto Gordo's lap, where she curled up like a happy house cat. "But I *am* sure he was the man in the car behind me when I drove over here to take pictures. He wore sunglasses and a tweed driving cap. The sunglasses were different from those at Nepenthe, but it was the same man."

"What make of car?"

"I couldn't tell in the rearview mirror. It was black. A compact, I think. I don't know. They all look alike to me."

"You're sure you'd never seen him before Nepenthe?"

"Positive. I don't man-watch like Cybil does, though I'm not one to overlook a man worth looking at if one crosses my path." She felt her cheeks warm and added,

"Cybil doesn't need her eyes examined where he's concerned."

Gordo absently stroked Squeeze's lower jaw and studied Rianna's troubled expression. "You don't have any ex-boyfriends who are Japanese, do you?"

"Gordon Nathan Davies," Rianna said reprovingly. "Would I provoke my own father into his second heart attack?"

He held up a hand as if to defend himself. "Just checking. I know your father never got over Pearl Harbor and our uncle Ned getting killed in the bombing. I just thought that with your artistic eye and your taste for the exotic, you—"

"These days," she cut in, "my taste for the exotic runs strictly to the portraits I paint of animals."

"It hasn't always run that way. Remember the Greek exchange student you went steady with in high school?" Gordo's blue eyes twinkled.

"Okay, okay," Rianna conceded. "Maybe I do—*did* have a weakness for foreign types, but Father never blinked an eye. A Japanese boyfriend, and he'd never speak to me again. So I've always limited my taste in things Japanese to sushi, sukiyaki and my red Subaru." She sighed. "For all his good looks, I'm getting edgy about this man popping up wherever I go."

"You look more than edgy," said Gordo, studying her with concern.

"I know. What if he's a psycho who gets obsessed with a woman, follows her and makes her life miserable? Every so often there's a newspaper headline or a magazine article about it."

"But what good can I do you at dinner?"

"A lot, I hope. If he's attracted, don't you think he'd get unattracted if he sees me with a date who stands six foot five and looks like you?"

Gordo considered that for a moment. "He might, but what if he's not at Casanova tonight?"

"He'll be there. I know it. I stopped in to make a reservation and while I was making it, he walked in and asked to see a menu for future reference."

"Have you seen him since?"

"He was feeding popcorn to a flock of pigeons on the sidewalk across the street from where I had my hair trimmed before I drove over here."

"Popcorn. Pigeons." Gordo shrugged and sat back. "Sounds harmless enough. He's probably just a tourist. I mean, he's never hassled you in any way from what you're saying."

"Isn't it enough that he's around every time I turn around?" she protested.

"I'd chalk it up to coincidence, but I can see you won't buy that." He regarded her with a perplexed expression. "Have you thought of going to the police about it?"

"Gordo, with a last name like Breece would *you* breathe a word of this to the police unless you absolutely, positively had to?"

"Nope. Not unless I wanted the news to leak out and hit the front page of the *National Enquirer* real quick."

"That's why I need you tonight," she pressed him. "I never want to make headlines coast-to-coast ever again. Remember how the reporters camped on your doorstep for a month, hoping you'd give them an exclusive about me?"

"Who could forget? Okay. I'm yours for dinner. You're sure this guy is medium height?"

"Positive. Why?"

"The coward in me wants to know, just in case he has a habit of punching his competition out."

"He's about five foot eleven. Eight inches taller than I am, but a shrimp next to you." It was best not to mention the suspect's broad shoulders and solid, muscular build.

"Those sound like reasonable odds for a cowardly high school basketball coach with more height than muscle," said Gordo, flexing his biceps. "Too bad we can't take Squeeze along to back me up."

THAT EVENING Casanova was packed. Two tables away from Rianna and Gordo, tough-guy movie star Kurt Westwood, Carmel's newest world-famed resident, had just been seated with a party of friends.

Over the top of the wine list she was scanning, Rianna's eyes widened in recognition. "He's here," she murmured to Gordo through her teeth. "He just came in."

Gordo stared back at her over the top of his menu. "You're sure it's him?"

"Yes. He's wearing a black-and-white-herringbone jacket. White shirt. Black slacks. Don't turn around. The host is seating him."

"Where?"

"Table for two right behind you. Facing me. He's alone. The busboy is taking away the second place setting. Try to get a good look at him."

"I can't without turning around."

"You can if you go to the rest room."

"Now?"

She nodded.

"But I—"

"Go right ahead, darling," she said in a normal tone, giving him a big, fake smile. "If the waiter comes back before you do, shall I order a zinfandel or a cabernet sauvignon?"

"Whatever your heart desires, uh, lover." Gordo pushed away from the table and stood. "I'll be back in a flash—my sweet."

Several diners, Kurt Westwood among them, looked up as Gordo passed through the room and ducked beneath the doorway. The reaction had been the same earlier when she and Gordo had been shown to their table. People took note of tall men. Rianna felt a rush of affection for her towering cousin. Tonight he'd worn a thick tweed sport coat over a bulky knit sweater to make himself look more like a bouncer and less like a basketball coach.

"You'll swelter in all that wool," Rianna had protested when he arrived at her place to pick her up.

"So? One look at me and your mystery man will break into a big sweat, too," had been Gordo's he-man reply.

From the admiring female glances and the envious male ones he was drawing, Rianna could see that the optical illusion was working. Was it having the same effect on the individual for whom it was intended?

Rianna glanced over the top of the wine list at the stranger. He was looking straight at her. His level gaze was one of cool appraisal, paired with what looked oddly like puzzlement. Though discomfited by his direct scrutiny, she met it.

He responded with a slight parting of his full, sensual lips. Was he tempted to speak to her?

Or kiss her?

Her heart stopped and she focused once more on the wine list. Kiss! Why was she conjuring up an image of this mysterious stranger kissing her as she stood at her easel, painting the provocative shape of his mouth?

"Have you decided, ma'am?"

Rianna looked up into a waiter's inquiring face. "What?"

"The wine. Or will the gentleman order when he returns?"

"Oh. No. I'll order." She stared yet again at the wine list. "Which cabernet can you recommend?"

"The '74 BV is excellent, or—"

"Perfect," she agreed before she could be flustered further by having to choose among several. "We'll have a bottle of the BV."

Was that a smug expression now on the handsome face at the opposite table? Rianna asked herself. She browsed through the dinner menu and occasionally glanced in his direction. He was smiling slightly to himself as he studied the wine list.

"Have you decided, sir?" she heard the same waiter ask him.

"What?"

Rianna was amazed to hear him sound just as distracted as she herself had been when asked the same question.

"The wine, sir. Are you ready to order?"

"Oh. Yes. Can you recommend a cabernet?"

One thing was certain. He was American-born. His voice was deep, unaccented with a husky timbre that made her want to hear him speak again. Realizing that his dialogue with the waiter was almost word for word what hers had been, Rianna risked another veiled glance at him. He had looked so smug only a moment ago. Was he mimicking her now? Making fun of her?

She suddenly wished she had dressed to the teeth instead of wearing a sedate teal-blue cashmere dress with long sleeves. It was easier to look haughty and untouchable in black silk, diamonds and spike heels. Especially if you were five foot three.

"As a matter of fact," the waiter responded, "the BV is excellent. We're serving it by the glass tonight, too."

Rianna stiffened. If he replied, "Perfect . . ."

"A glass it is, then," she heard him say.

She averted her eyes and mentally reviewed his appearance. He was clean-shaven, his skin smooth, almost luminous. His white shirt, with cuffs sporting square silver cuff links, was open at the neck. His straight black hair was swept back and grazed the top of his collar. His expression during his exchange with the waiter had been polite and intelligent.

"Psychotic" was the last word that came to Rianna's mind when she considered what his demeanor suggested. "Confident" was the first, and "competent, calm and composed" followed.

Who was he and what did he want? Was *she* being paranoid?

She reviewed what Gordo has shrugged off as coincidence. Nepenthe. The post office. The art-supply shop. The route to Gordo's place in nearby Monterey. Casanova. Then again, a Carmel tourist *could* find himself at any or all of those locations during a few days' stay, couldn't he?

She welcomed Gordo's return with a smile of relief—and a slight pang of guilt. Had she brought him here to discourage a man who might not have the faintest idea she was alive, much less care? After Chloe, Squeeze-Play and basketball, a poker night with his buddies was Gordo's favorite pastime. Casanova couldn't begin to compare.

"WHAT'S HE DOING NOW?" Gordo muttered after their meal was finished and brandy and coffee had been served.

"Putting his credit card back in his wallet," Rianna murmured. "He's signed the check. He's putting his wallet in his—" She sucked in a breath. "Oh, my God!"

Gordo's big blue eyes grew perfectly round, mirroring the sudden alarm she felt. "What?"

"Shh. He's—he's standing up."

"You look ready to scream."

"Hush, here he comes." She touched her brandy glass to Gordo's as the object of their attention came around his table in their direction. "Darling man," she cooed at her cousin, loud enough for the stranger to hear. "You're spending the night, aren't you, tiger?"

Gordo gulped. "Spending the—? Oh, you bet I am. Every night from now on, gorgeous. Grrr."

Torn between mounting terror of the man who seemed to hesitate before he walked past, and chagrin at her mild-mannered cousin's anemic imitation of a predatory male, Rianna held her seductive smile and pose.

"He's gone," Gordo said after a few seconds. "Out the door. I saw him turn right and walk past the window. What happened when he stood up? You looked like Dracula had attacked and drained you dry."

"Oh, Gordo." Rianna set her brandy down and put fear-chilled hands to her cheeks. Her eyes filled with tears. "If he really is following me, I'm in big trouble."

"Rianna, all he's done tonight is eat dinner in the same restaurant. Calm down."

"I can't. Now that I know he's—" She broke off and wrapped her arms around herself, feeling terrified.

"Look, he's done nothing," Gordo soothed. "He's said nothing. He never approached our table or looked at either of us cross-eyed even once tonight. He's well-dressed and has the refinement and good taste to dine in the best places. You're imagining things."

"I am *not*. I'm not imagining what I saw when he put his wallet in his breast pocket."

"What?"

"His gun!"

2

"WHATEVER YOU DO, don't call me a dumb blonde with an overactive imagination—even if I fit the description tonight," Rianna groused as Gordo walked her to the door of her cottage after their stop at the Carmel police station. "How could I know that any man toting a gun at Casanova tonight had to be one of Kurt Westwood's bodyguards?"

"Don't kick yourself over it, Rianna. It didn't cross my mind, either. Not until the sergeant asked if anything unusual had been going on at Casanova, and I said Westwood was there."

"I wonder how many bodyguards he has?"

"You heard the sergeant. More than one. Enough to discourage the women and autograph hounds."

"I wish I'd grasped the obvious connection when the Westwood group left the restaurant just after the gunslinger did," Rianna fretted. "I feel ridiculous, rushing to the police to file a concealed-weapons report. Please, God, don't let any of it hit the news media tomorrow."

"The sergeant looked like a man to be trusted."

Rianna grimaced and shrugged. "I hope so. I'd hate to read in the papers tomorrow about what a dimwit I've been tonight."

"Don't worry," Gordo said calmly. "He promised to forget you'd been to the station, remember? And he was nice enough to thank you for doing your duty as a concerned citizen."

"We'll see. And speaking of thanks, have I thanked *you* for being the most concerned cousin and one of the best friends I've ever had, Gordo?"

He grinned down at her. "What's a cousin for if he can't show a little friendly concern now and then? How often do I get to swagger around like Arnold Schwarzenegger and stuff myself with a swank dinner?"

"About as often as you'll be out doing pizza and poker with the guys after you marry Chloe."

"Chloe's worth it."

Rianna laughed and handed him the bulky tweed sport coat he'd draped over her shoulders against the chill of the April evening. "Thanks again, Gordo. Goodnight."

He waited until she stepped inside. "You sure you'll be okay now? You can sleep at my place if the jitters have gotten to be a habit."

Rianna held out a rock-steady hand. "What jitters?"

HE WAS in the middle of a hamstring stretch when she left her shingled cottage the next morning. Screened from her view by a juniper hedge, he continued his prejog warm-up and kept an eye on her.

As she'd done the past three mornings, she latched the wooden gate to her high-walled front yard and jogged down the sidewalk at a leisurely pace. It disappointed him that she was wearing scarlet sweats this foggy Sunday morning.

He'd liked her best in the aqua running tights and matching cropped T-shirt she'd worn yesterday. Now, after seeing her gaze close up at Casanova the night before, he knew why. With her creamy complexion, curly blond hair and turquoise eyes, all shades and blends of blue and green were a perfect complement.

He could see, though, why she'd bundled up today. Fog swirled all around, driven by chilly gusts of wind. He had opted for heavyweight gray sweats with a hood this morning to stay both warm and inconspicuous. Pale gray in this fog was perfect. So was scarlet, for his purpose.

When she was far enough ahead, he pulled the hood over his hair and jogged after her. Keeping her slim figure in view, he followed her down the tree-lined streets and narrow alleyways of residential Carmel to the sidewalk promenade that skirted a stretch of Carmel Beach. What was it about her that made him feel he'd met her before, when he hadn't? He'd never met her before. He was positive of that.

As he tailed her, he mulled over how he had almost blown everything by following her too closely yesterday. Dining at Casanova had been overkill. He'd known it the minute she'd flicked him that glance of recognition and started flirting openly and outrageously with her cousin.

Whatever else they were, he already knew Rianna Breece and Gordon Davies were not lovers. That was a fact. He had researched his target's background and life-style in great detail before beginning the stakeout. And after three days of monitoring her daily routine, he knew even more.

It would have been easier if he hadn't found himself overwhelmed by the first sight of her at Nepenthe. Nor had the double rainbow that arched over the scene helped him in his struggle to remain cool and objective. No, the snapshots and news clippings in his file on Rianna Breece hadn't prepared him for her creamy complexion or astonishing eyes. He'd known she was petite, but hadn't expected her slim, fine-boned frame to be fleshed out with high, firm breasts, womanly hips and the sleek, toned thighs of a dedicated daily jogger.

A delicate flaxen blonde, a gifted artist, wealthy and attractive—she appeared to have it all. All but peace of mind and a man in her life. The last of her few involvements had been dashing but destitute Brent Halston, her former fiancé. On the day of their wedding a year ago, Brent had boarded the supersonic Concorde in New York with a comely French countess far wealthier than Rianna. She and five hundred dearly beloved guests waited in vain at the church for the groom who had jilted her.

Her father, a newspaper publisher and heir to a California publishing fortune, had reportedly been on the verge of a heart attack at the sight of the snickering headlines in rival newspapers.

The man following Rianna stared ahead at her and thought of the sensationalistic headlines and biased editorials that Nathan Breece's papers were notorious for. With those in mind, it was a simpler task to check any rush of sympathy for the woman Halston had abandoned. To all appearances she had survived her fiancé's defection, headlines and all. Whether she had healed as well as survived was another matter.

Whatever the case, there had been no romance in her life since that humiliation on her wedding day. He refused to examine why he was pleased by that fact. It was simply a lucky break. A man in Rianna Breece's life would only have complicated things.

His job was complex enough now that she had somehow caught on that he was tracking her. Worst of all, she had seen the gun. Damn! He wished he'd been concentrating on details other than the way she pressed her lips to her wineglass or how her breasts tilted under the cashmere of her dress. It wasn't like him to forget about the revolver in its underarm holster. Still, a friendly midnight chat with the sergeant at the police station had confirmed the reason for her visit. His lips twisted in a wry smile of thanks to Kurt Westwood for dining in town. Another lucky break.

He stepped up his pace to gain on Rianna as she neared Carmel Beach. Before she reached it, he'd make his move.

Rianna checked her watch. A nine-minute mile. Way to go. Her rhythmic pace and respiration had an almost hypnotic power over her. *Fog.* She'd never been able to fully master the technique required to capture it in oil paints.

She shivered, not at the chill, but because the Monterey pines lining the route were so beautiful she felt a sudden compulsion to retrace the route to her cottage and paint fog-laced pines this morning. She suppressed the desire, knowing she would pay dearly if she didn't run the entire three miles. Otherwise her insomnia would be even worse. It didn't help at all to remember that before Brent and those sneering headlines, she'd slept like a babe.

Now, just to be assured of a mere four hours' uninterrupted sleep, she had to run, swim, hike or bike or endure the agony of tossing and turning in search of the rest that would not come. Last night, however, relieved that she wasn't being followed, she had slept the night through for the first time in a year.

All the same, the fog was alluring. Rianna couldn't escape the longing to express in paint the emotions it evoked in her. She debated whether one mile out and one back would do the trick. Then she made a tight U-turn and saw him.

Wearing hooded gray sweats, he was running after her, straight out of the mist. She froze, first from fear, then in paralyzing confusion. Was this just another coincidence?

"Miss Breece!" he called out.

He knew her name! His was the same deep voice she'd first heard the night before. He was no coincidental tourist.

Run, she urged herself. *Run for your life.* She twirled and sprinted at full speed away from him.

"Hold it!" she heard him call. "Wait up!"

From behind came the slap-slap of his shoes as he reduced the distance between them on the damp sidewalk of the promenade. Ahead of her lay the most popular section of Carmel Beach and the safety of the parking area. Cars and people were always there. It was regularly patrolled by the police. If only she could reach it before he—

"Miss . . . Breece . . ."

He sounded almost as winded as she felt. And closer. Only a few steps behind her. Oh, God. The blood in her thigh and calf muscles burned. Her lungs were on fire.

"Leave . . . me . . . alone!" she gasped over her shoulder.

"Just . . . stop . . . for . . . a . . . sec," he gasped back, coming abreast of her right shoulder.

Panic swelled in her throat. Out of the corner of her eye she could see that his body would block any angled sprint she might make toward the row of houses that lined the promenade. Unless she could outrun him, she was trapped between him and the ocean.

"Let's . . . talk," he panted.

"No!"

He pulled slightly ahead. "Please . . ."

She shook her head, unable to utter another word. The parking lot was little more than a hundred yards away.

"Stop—" He touched her arm.

She threw off his hand and pulled two paces ahead of him, heading for the parking lot. There she saw a police patrol car. The officer was leaning against it, talking to an older couple who stood next to a gigantic Winnebago. She headed straight for him, frantically waving her arms.

"Help! Help! Please . . ."

Three faces turned in her direction, registering surprise.

"That man—" She puffed as she skidded to a stop. "He's—"

Surprise turned to alarm as the three looked over her shoulder. The officer made the first move. He rushed past her in the direction from which she'd come. Before she could gasp any further plea for help, the older couple trotted after him.

"Oh, my," she heard the woman say. "That poor young man."

"He's out cold," the man added.

Rianna whipped around to stare after them. Her pursuer lay motionless, facedown on the sidewalk just a few yards from the spot where she had pulled ahead. She didn't see the long, bloody gash on his forehead until she sped back to where he lay and watched the burly officer ease him onto his back.

"Whoa, there. Well, damned if it isn't Ty. . . ! Hey, Tyler T! What are you doing in town without looking me up for a beer?" the officer inquired, patting the man's blood-streaked cheek. "You okay, you clumsy flatfoot?"

Rianna stared at the officer; she remembered him now from a speeding ticket he'd given her a year ago.

Gallagher was his name. Her insurance premiums had gone up twenty percent. Had he said *Ty? Tyler T?* She turned her attention to the man on the ground. He struggled to sit up, looking so hurt and helpless that she felt a momentary urge to cradle his broad shoulders in her arms and stroke back the shock of black hair from his bloodied forehead.

"Officer," she said, checking that impulse, "do you know this man?"

"Sure." He looked up at her. "Don't you?"

"No.... I've only seen him around...here and there. Who is he?"

"A good buddy. I've known Ty since sixth grade. We were rookie cops in San Francisco together. I thought you were running with him."

"I—"

"Say, didn't I nail you doing forty-five in a thirty-five last year?"

"Uh...yes."

"Thought so. Red Subaru. Breece, right?"

"Er, right. You're Officer Gallagher, right?"

"On the nose. Ms. Breece, if you don't know him, why were you running with him?"

"I wasn't. He just happened to be behind me."

"Oh. Well, it was a good thing you saw him fall and ran for help when you—"

A low groan interrupted the policeman. "Stay down until your head settles, Ty," the officer suggested. "You're gonna need a stitch or six from the size of that split. Still, you never were much of a bleeder. Looks like nothing's changed." He dabbed at the cut with his handkerchief. "You on vacation again, guy?"

"Biff?" Ty inquired, his voice sounding groggy.

"The one and only. How you ended up facedown is a better question."

Ty winced and squeezed his eyes shut. "Damned tree root tripped me."

Gallagher chuckled and helped him sit up while Rianna and the older couple hovered over the two. "Yeah, blame it on Mother Nature. Bet you were chasing this beautiful blonde, here," he said with a wink at Rianna.

"Help me up, Biff."

"Take it easy, now," the officer advised as he assisted him to his feet. "I'll run you over to Emergency after you get steady."

"I can make it." Ty swayed slightly and gazed unsteadily at the three pairs of eyes that were fixed on him. He focused on Rianna. "I meant no harm," he murmured.

"I'm . . . sorry," she said haltingly. "I—I didn't know you were on the—" she gestured at the officer "—the right side of the law."

"Tyler Toranaga on the right side of the law?" Officer Gallagher threw back his head and laughed. "Only when he's lifting a beer side by side with me, right, good buddy?"

"Only half-right," Ty replied with a flash of humor in his dark eyes. "The rest of the time I'm beating the police to the punch with my own footwork."

"You could always go back to being one of Frisco's best," Gallagher said. "I hear the chief's ulcers haven't been the same since you left. He misses his daily bottle of Maalox. The guys say he'd love it if you'd reenlist."

"The chief might, but *I* wouldn't. I like being my own boss."

Gallagher shook his head. "Once a loner, always a loner. What can I say?"

"Tell Miss Breece I'm a private investigator from San Francisco who's licensed to carry a gun."

"That he is," the officer confirmed. "But why?"

"Investigating what?" Rianna inquired, settling her hands on her hips at the unwelcome news that he was a private eye. *Toranaga.* Why did the name ring a bell?

Ty glanced at the curious older couple. "Perhaps we could discuss that over dinner at La Playa tonight?"

Rianna dug in her heels. "Who hired you to follow me around, Mr. Toranaga?" *Ah, yes.* Toranaga had been the name of a character in James Clavell's novel, *Shogun.*

"My client wishes to remain nameless at this time," he replied.

"Nameless. Why?"

"We could best discuss *that* tonight, too. Is eight o'clock convenient?"

"Why have you been dogging my heels for three days?" she persisted.

"You weren't supposed to know I was doing that. What tipped you off to me?"

"Try answering a few of *my* questions first."

"I believe I offered to do that at dinner."

She met his adamant attitude with one equally unyielding. "Dinner at La Playa doesn't come cheap. Your client must have deep pockets."

"If my client can't afford it, I can."

"Tell me who you're working for and I'll consider it."

His eyes flicked to Gallagher. "Vouch for me, would you, Biff?"

The officer readily complied. "He's A-okay. The best private eye around. And if you ever need a bodyguard, he's a black belt at karate."

Rianna blinked. "Bodyguard?"

"You bet. Why, he—"

"That'll do, Biff," Ty cut in uneasily.

"Bodyguard," Rianna muttered, and then widened her eyes in sudden realization. "So *that's* it." Her indignation blazed hotter. "I never thought he'd go so far as to . . ." She scrunched her damp curls with the fingers of one hand and laid into Ty. "If my father hired you as my bodyguard you can stop guarding my body right now. I've told him a million times that I refuse to live like a rich, paranoid—"

Ty held up a hand, his eyes as frozen as hers felt fiery. "Nathan Breece is the last man on earth I'd ever work for. Nor is his daughter's body one I'd hire out to guard unless I was forced."

"Hey, Ty," Gallagher muttered. "Ease up, hotshot. She's a fine, upstanding member of this communi—"

"Thank you, officer, but I can speak for myself." Rianna turned on Ty. "Your extreme lack of tact is precisely what I'd expect of a man who pries into the private lives of others for a living. Now that you've insulted my father behind his back and me to my face, please be advised that I refuse to dine with you."

"I'm sorry I said that. It was thoughtless." *Thoughtless but true,* he added to himself. He needed her cooperation, though. "Please forgive me. If dinner tonight isn't convenient, can we meet sometime tomorrow? I desperately need your help for what I can only say is a good cause."

"I see. If you're soliciting funds for charity, you should contact my—"

"I'm not. I'll answer your questions—and calm your fears."

She stood silently sizing him up, then yielded when his sincere expression and her own intense curiosity won out over indignation.

"Very well. I'll be there tonight on one condition."

"Name it."

"When you dress for dinner, don't wear your gun."

He lifted an eyebrow. "What if I do? Do you intend to frisk me at the table?"

"Your word is enough. I hate firearms of all shapes and sizes."

He looked surprised. "Nathan Breece's newspapers have fought every gun-control law ever proposed."

"I may be my father's daughter, Mr. Toranaga, but I'm not his puppet. I'll agree to dinner only if your gun stays home. I hope I've made my point."

"You've scored a bull's-eye, Miss Breece. I'll pick you up a little before eight."

"No, you won't. I love to walk. Since I live within walking distance of La Playa, I'll meet you there."

"No, you won't," he replied with a conviction that matched hers. "I'll meet you on your doorstep and walk with you."

"Don't you ever do anything other than your way?"

"Yes. I sometimes compromise. You see, I hate to walk."

"Don't make the trek to my doorstep then. I'll meet you at the front gate."

"HOW DOES the rack of lamb for two sound to you?" Ty inquired.

"Delicious. I was about to ask you the same thing," Rianna replied. "How do you like yours?"

"Medium. And you?"

"The same. It's the first thing we've agreed on since this morning."

"It'll be two if you like zinfandel."

"Make it two."

Ty settled back in his chair and popped one of the three olives from his martini on the rocks into his mouth. Once again something elusively familiar nudged at his memory as he regarded Rianna with an appraising eye. She couldn't have dressed more attractively had she known he favored the blue-green tones that intensified the turquoise of her eyes. Her dress tonight was of aqua silk, her lips a pearlescent pink, her hair a flaxen halo of light.

Her dress and coloring reminded him of the double rainbow at Nepenthe, but she couldn't know he had a thing about rainbows. Nor could she know that the sight of tiny diamond chips studding her earlobes would make him feel suddenly light-headed at the thought of warming them with his tongue.

I could paint a stunning portrait of him, Rianna thought as she sipped her Campari. She tried to concentrate on the questions she had come to ask rather than on Ty and the arresting angles of his cheekbones and brows, the tantalizing shape of his mouth and eyes, the crisp white of his shirt, the onyx black of his suit and hair. His strong, long-fingered hands, too, were designed for life-study sketching. The silver ring on the third finger of his left hand was wide and plain. A wedding ring?

"Are you married, Mr. Toranaga?" she blurted.

"I was hoping to dispense with the formalities before we got started tonight." He pulled a business card out of his shirt pocket and handed it to her. "Tyler Toranaga. I go by Ty, Rianna."

Rianna examined the card. "So you work out of San Francisco," she observed. "What part of the city?"

"Potrero Hill. But you're getting ahead of me with the questions. I haven't answered your first one."

"I shouldn't have asked it. It's none of my business, is it?" She bit her lip and sat up straighter. "I have an old friend, a sculptor, who has a studio on Potrero Hill.

I've been there several times. Do you live on the hill as well as keeping an office there?"

"I live nearby. Your friend wouldn't happen to be Eric Nordstrom, the brass sculptor, would he?"

"Why, yes. You know him, too?" Rianna's attention was piqued by the name. She leaned forward with interest.

Ty nodded. "I bought one of his pieces a few years ago when his work was still affordable." His heart sank as he recalled the tall sculptor's superb build, Scandinavian good looks and reputation for wowing the ladies.

"Really? What a coincidence. I've bought from him, too." Rianna clasped her hands and settled her chin on them. "What did you buy? He sends me color slides of everything he does."

Annoyed that he'd mentioned the godlike Viking, Ty waved a hand and shrugged. "It's a minor piece. An investment, really. Nothing compared to what you've collected, I'm sure."

"Nothing Eric does is minor," Rianna said firmly. "Tell me."

"We're not here to talk sculpture, Miss—"

"Rianna," she cut in, wagging a finger at him. "No formalities and no evading the question. I've bought *Maelstrom One*, *Maelstrom Three* and *Ecstasy in Motion*. The first two are on loan to the Met for a special exhibit next month. Now you."

She had named three of Nordstrom's most provocative and emotionally charged nude figures. Two were male, one female. Ty wondered why his research hadn't turned up this aspect of Rianna Breece's artistic tastes. If it had, he'd never have admitted to owning a Nordstrom. He couldn't imagine what had prompted him to reveal the fact in the first place. Now that he'd sprung off the high dive, though, he figured headfirst was the only way to go. Especially with Rianna's expectant stare pinned on him.

"I bought *Hope,*" he said, gulping down his martini, "and I've never loaned it out. Are you familiar with *Hope?*"

Rianna saw the tinge of dull red that stained his cheekbones. At the same instant she felt her own cheeks drain of all color.

"Hope." Her voice cracked. She cleared her throat. "Yes.... I think so...."

"As I said, it's nothing compared to the two *Maelstroms.* And now that we've inventoried our sculpture collections," he continued in obvious haste, "the answer to your first question is no, I'm not married. I was, once...for two years a long time ago. No kids. Since my amicable divorce, I've been what Biff Gallagher called me this morning—a loner."

Relieved that he had so quickly changed the subject, Rianna finished off her Campari in a single swallow. "I'm sorry I brought it up," she apologized again. "It certainly wasn't one of the questions I came here to ask."

"Ask."

"Why have you been following me?"

"My client is a nonprofit organization for the protection and preservation of endangered wildlife species." He named a famous society. "The organization has long known that rare animals are being smuggled into this country from all over the world by wealthy, unscrupulous breeders, collectors, sportsmen."

"I've read about that in the papers," she reflected, "but I'm not really up on the subject."

"It's not pleasant, Rianna. While some of the breeders believe the countries of origin aren't succeeding in their protection or preservation efforts and so claim that smuggling them to the U.S. is for the sake of the species, others smuggle animals in for their valuable fur and horns. Exotic birds are in great demand, as are rare reptiles and their skins." Ty's mouth hardened. "Some mammals are even brought in for sport hunters to slaughter on domestic safaris."

"They're hunted down as trophies?"

Tyler nodded. "To be stuffed and mounted and pointed to with macho pride. Hundreds of animals every year. Sick, isn't it?"

"Yes.... I've heard talk of such things, of course, in the course of my work for exotic animal owners. But I never suspected it was more than a few animals a year. Hundreds, you say?"

"That's a conservative government estimate. The organization's research indicates animals are coming in illegally by the thousands. In fact— Here's the waiter."

They ordered French onion soup, salad and lamb. After the waiter left them, Ty continued with a barrage of statistics that Rianna admitted sounded alarming.

"What's the government doing about it?" she asked after Ty had checked off the most distressing of the numbers.

"With an unprecedented surge of drugs coming into this country by air, land and sea, what do *you* think it's doing about a few thousand animals?"

"I see the problem." Rianna toyed with her salad fork. "But you still haven't explained why you followed me."

"Bear with me. First you should know that I volunteer what time I can spare to the organization. In the past two years I've done enough investigating to prove a ring of smugglers is operating here in the Monterey-Carmel area."

"Have you informed the authorities?"

"Yes."

"And. . . ?"

"My proof's sitting there in the stacks of cases they don't yet have the time or money to investigate. So I'm pushing ahead with my own investigation on my own time. I'm able to spare a month out of my work schedule right now without going into bankruptcy."

Rianna watched him unconsciously flex his hand into a fist. The conviction he brought to his efforts on behalf of animals was admirable.

"I'm impressed," she declared, "but where do *I* fit into all this?"

"I'm fairly certain you've unknowingly painted portraits of at least one of the animals I'm talking about. I'd like to see any preliminary sketches or slides of commissioned portraits you might have in your files."

"That's all you need from me? Why didn't you just phone and say what you've just told me, instead of tracking me for three days like a hunted animal?"

She had to wait until their soup was served before Ty answered. "You've been under surveillance for longer than three days, Rianna. I assigned one of my men—Al—to watch you starting three months ago."

"You mean . . . long before this, I . . . ?"

"I know it's maddening, but I had to make sure you weren't one of the smugglers."

"You suspected me?"

He shrugged. "I had to. You paint exotics. You've earned a reputation for your work as far away as Europe. Who's to say an artist wouldn't conspire to smuggle in the rarest of animal species that could be painted right here in her own backyard? In my line of work, you learn to suspect everyone until they prove innocent."

"But who . . . ? I never knew I was being watched until a few days ago."

Ty's expression and tone turned grave as he said, "You wouldn't have known even now if I'd been as good as Al. When did you figure out I was following you, by the way?"

"At Nepenthe. My friend Cybil who was with me... She, er, keeps an eye out for exceptional-looking men."

He colored slightly. "I see. And you don't."

"Not like Cybil does." It was her turn to flush. "She's not shy."

"She wouldn't even have noticed me if I'd been Al," he said ruefully. He stabbed his toothpick into the last olive in his martini, feeling absurd for wishing he'd caught Rianna's eye first. "He was as nondescript as a guy can get and twice as honest and discreet. The best surveillance man I had."

"Had?"

"Yeah." Ty drew a breath that shook and held it until he could say with only a slight tremor, "He was murdered a week ago."

3

MURDERED!

Rianna's spoon slid with a clang from her fingers into her soup bowl. Stricken, she stared at Ty.

Ty waited for the hum of voices to resume before he squared his shoulders and continued. "Al called in that morning and said he was on to something big. Said he'd drive up to the office to file his most recent notes and bring in a roll of film he'd shot of an animal delivery in a cove near Big Sur. He got as close as a parking space in front of the office. I heard the shot and ran down. He was slumped over the steering wheel with a note taped on his back. There was no sign of the film or his file in the car."

"What did the note say?"

"'Lay off, or—'" he paused as if deciding something "'—or else.'"

"Lay off what?"

"Good question. Al and I worked together a few years back on a narcotics case. The local drug dealer we nailed was released on parole last weekend and I'd bet solid gold he's back dealing again. Knowing him, the motive could easily have been revenge."

"If it was, you could be in danger, too."

Ty shrugged. "I don't think so. Al played the heavy in that case. There's a slim chance this may have nothing to do with that sleazy punk."

"And everything to do with the animal smugglers?"

"As I said, chances are slim."

"Ty, if the killer meant for you to lay off the smuggling investigation, you could be in danger here in Carmel."

"Not likely. You see, I've vacationed at La Playa in April for the past two years, never working the case during that time. I've done nothing in the last three days to make anyone think I'm not the yearly vacationer I've always been. Besides, no one is tailing me. I've done enough surveillance work to know if there's a watchful eye around. No one is tailing *you* either, right now."

"But you think someone might, right? That whoever shot Al might come after me?"

"There's only the slimmest of chances," he reminded her. "I'm almost certain nothing in Al's notes spelled out any connection with you, but I'm not positive. Until I am, I'll stick close to make sure you're safe. And while I'm at it, I want to examine your sketches and slides."

"But if someone *should* be following me around, we shouldn't be meeting here in the open. It looks as if we're up to something, and we are."

Ty shook his head. "You're not thinking like a spy. If we had ulterior motives, why would we meet in public for everyone to see? And you're forgetting about this." He indicated the bandage on his forehead. "Look at things the way a private eye does. Anyone tracking either of us would have seen me fall. He would have seen you run for help. Now he sees me thanking you for it with dinner at my hotel. I'm single, you're single. What man doesn't have a weakness for a beautiful, sexy blonde?"

"Ty, I'm not—"

"You *are* both, and I'm not finished. From all outward appearances we met by accident, the attraction was mutual and nature is taking its course. If you invite me back to your place after dinner, that just reinforces it. Even *I* couldn't work up a case for collusion after watching *that* scenario unfold."

Ty knew he'd been right to play things cool and confident with her. He'd been right, too, in withholding what the last part of the threat had actually been. He'd decide after dinner whether to tell her that the message had been "Lay off, or she's next." Though in truth, he himself wasn't sure whether "she" referred to Rianna or the former addict who had tipped off the police about her dealer's illegal activities.

Whatever he did, Ty knew he had to spend every day with Rianna until he was certain she had nothing to fear. After losing Al, he wasn't putting anyone's life on the line but his own.

APPROACHING Rianna's front door, Ty commented with a wry smile, "From the outside, your cottage looks like something the Brothers Grimm might have dreamed up."

Rianna laughed softly. "You're close. The previous owner was an author who specialized in fairy tales. 'Enchanted' was the word the realtor used when he described it to me over the phone. I bought it on first sight a few months ago, rainbows and all."

"Rainbows?" Ty stumbled slightly on the perfectly smooth path from the gate to her door.

"Watch your step and keep an open mind." She unlocked the door and switched on a light. "Welcome to my little corner of Oz."

Ty stepped into a small living room luminous with the prismatic hues of the rainbow. Pastel-tinted frescoes on each of the four white-plastered walls depicted rainbowed seascapes. A window on the west wall had been shaped to frame arched bands of stained glass with the same motif. A white cotton couch and chairs were banked with fat, multihued, tie-dyed pillows.

Ty's appraising gaze swept the room and returned to Rianna. The tints of her silk dress, her hair, her eyes, each was more luminous than any color in the room. To Ty she was a more dazzling phenomenon than any rainbow he'd ever seen. More than any woman he'd ever known, she seemed to wrap her own special enchantment around each moment he spent with her.

"I . . . it's . . . I'm . . ."

"Just lie and say you're charmed," she suggested dryly. "You'll set yourself apart from the rest who've said rainbows are cute—for women, kids and wimps."

"Who was crass enough to say that?"

"Not you. Not yet."

"Maybe never. Maybe I'm a wimp."

"And I'm Rambo IV," she retorted. "Stick with saying you're charmed even if it's not what you're thinking."

If he said what he was thinking, she'd never believe it. He remembered his grandmother telling him as a small boy, "Wishes on rainbows are wishes come true." From that moment he'd been hooked. He'd kept every wish a secret in his heart and most of them had come true. Tell that, even to a woman with five rainbows in her living room? He might chase rainbows but he wasn't crazy.

He chose instead to change the subject and said, "Looking around, I can't help wondering why Nathan Breece's daughter lives in a storybook cottage rather than the family mansion on Seventeen-Mile Drive."

"And I wonder why everyone always assumes I live on the huge trust fund everyone read about in the papers when Brent left me high and dry."

Ty raised an eyebrow in genuine surprise. "Don't you?"

"No. My cousin Gordo and I are the black sheep in the family. He's a teacher and I paint for a living," she said, her tone edged with a hint of frost. "I've never touched my trust fund. One bedroom, one office, one bath and a garage converted into a studio is all the house I can afford in Carmel by the Sea. I realize I could live elsewhere with more space and a smaller mortgage, but this is my home town. My studio is right this way."

Chastised, Ty followed where she led. "I see you like oak antiques and old books as well as rainbows," he observed in an attempt to dispel the chill between them. "So do I."

He was rewarded with a lessening of her reserve. "They came with the house when I bought it," she replied. "I moved my clothes in and voilà! Antiques, books and rainbows. I was home."

She led him through a small kitchen crowded with potted plants to her studio and turned on the lights. The scent of turpentine and oil paint permeated the air. Three walls of the spacious room were lined with large, deep cubbyholes, each filled with sketches and labeled with the species of animal it contained.

"Is that what it looks like it is?" Ty asked with a shudder at the half-finished painting on the easel in the middle of the room.

"If it looks like something named Squeeze-Play, it is. She's ten feet of pure python with not a mean bone in her body, unless you're a hunk of ham or a mouse and it's dinnertime."

"I can think of more appetizing entrées."

"Me, too. The lamb tonight was delicious."

"So was the company," he stunned himself by saying. When had his tongue decided to do its own thing?

"Why, thank you." She turned to conceal the flush his unbidden compliment had raised in her cheeks, then added, "I enjoyed yours, too." She kept her back to him and contemplated the nearest wall of cubbyholes.

"Where do you want to start? Llamas, macaws, mongooses—or is it mongeese?"

"Could we start with Irish coffees first? The two you wouldn't let me order for us after dinner?" Amazed that his tongue had again severed its connection to his brain, he decided he must have had one too many rainbows tonight. The last thing he needed was an Irish coffee to cloud what last vestige of reason he might yet own.

As things stood, a man of his well-justified objections to the prejudices of the father should be sticking strictly to business with the daughter. He shouldn't be wondering what she'd do if he kissed her.

Rianna turned to face him, aware that she shouldn't welcome the extended rapport an after-dinner drink promised, yet welcoming it just the same. There was no sense in cultivating this disturbing attraction to Ty. There was even less sense in overlooking his Japanese heritage and her father's long-standing prejudice.

"I'm out of whipped cream, I'm afraid," she hedged.

"You're not out of milk. That'll do." Too late, he bit his tongue. Her eyes were already narrowing.

"How do *you* know I'm not out of milk?"

"I—a wild guess."

"Wild my Aunt Penelope. Did you see me buy milk at the grocery store after I left Gordo's yesterday?"

"Uh . . . yeah . . . sort of."

"Sort of?"

"Okay. I did. You bought milk, cheese, cold cuts and a quart of sherbet."

"How did you—? Damn, why didn't I catch you there? Where were you hiding?"

"Nowhere. I was in disguise."

"What disguise?"

"A sleuth never tells."

She settled her palms upon her hips and squared off at him. "You even know what flavor of sherbet I bought, don't you?" It was hard to remain indignant, though, now that she'd remembered the tampons she'd purchased at the same time. Gallant and thoughtful of him not to mention them.

He gave her a pleading smile. "It looked like rainbow from where I was standing. If it was, I can say I know why."

"Cute. It was. Tell me, is there anything worth knowing that you don't already know about me?"

"I didn't know about the rainbows," he offered, his smile a hopeful plea for mercy.

"As far as the critics are concerned, those aren't *worth* knowing about."

"Does it help that I also didn't know you pay your own bills?"

"Only slightly. I didn't know the Internal Revenue Service could keep a secret."

"Would it help more if I said I admire a work ethic in a woman with a trust fund worth millions?" he pursued, exaggerating his appeasing smile.

"Only slightly more." She turned toward the kitchen, unable to stop herself surrendering a smile to his. "Do you take decaffeinated or regular in your Bushmills?"

"I'll take whatever you do. You're the insomniac."

She didn't want to know how he knew that.

A few minutes later they settled onto the pillowed couch, sipping the whiskey-laced brew from slim glass cups and listening to soft jazz on the stereo.

Ty found himself fantasizing about Rianna, rainbows and romance and mentally cursing his train of thought. Had her last name been any other, had this been a simple dinner date with any other woman, he knew what he'd be doing right now. He'd be spending the night at her invitation instead of contemplating how to announce he was staying overnight with or without it.

"How long have you been working on your own?" Rianna asked during the first pause in the music.

"Five years. I quit the force when I was twenty-seven and never looked back."

He looked so grim as he said it that Rianna decided she wouldn't inquire what his reasons had been. Then, recalling his probing questions earlier, she decided to do some probing of her own.

"Why?"

"You don't want to know."

"You know more about me than it'll ever be fair for anyone to know. What don't I want to know?"

"A lot. Some of San Francisco's streets are meaner than anyone from your side of the tracks has ever seen. An undercover cop sees every gritty detail up close and personally when he walks a beat."

"You worked undercover in the city?"

Ty nodded. "Long enough to get out before it ate me alive. Gallagher and I worked a narcotics squad together. He quit right after I did."

"Why?"

"His wife threatened to leave him and take the kids with her. He saw the light and bailed out to come down here and work nine to five. Now they're one big, happy family."

She noticed he hadn't included his own reasons for quitting. "What about *you*, Ty?" she prodded. "Are you happy in your work?"

"For the most part, yes. My partner and I employ several industrial security specialists in the Silicon Valley, and we have two bodyguards who protect local and visiting celebrities and socialites from mobs on special occasions."

"Al wasn't your partner?"

"No. He was a free-lancer doing me a big favor." Ty squeezed his eyes shut. "Too big a favor. I miss him, dammit. I wish I could be at his funeral, but...well, his folks will understand. His father beat the sidewalks of San Francisco for thirty years before he retired from the troops."

"Why can't you be at the funeral?"

Ty swallowed a long draught of his drink, set his cup upon the coffee table and turned to Rianna. "Because my job right now is here, making sure you're safe."

Rianna put down her cup next to Ty's with a trembling hand. "You said I wasn't in any—"

"I said that because we'd established a rapport over dinner I hadn't expected. I enjoyed being with you too much to want to roll in the heavy artillery before dessert." He caught her hand in his and held it firmly. "It seemed best to wait until later to tell you."

"Tell me what?"

"That I think you should have a bodyguard until I figure out what's up."

Her hand clutched his. "At dinner you said chances were slim that I might be—"

"They are right now," he cut in. "Tomorrow could be another story. I'll know for sure after I comb through your slides and sketches."

"For what?"

"Faces of people in the background—photos or sketches you have of pet owners, anything that might match a description of one of the smugglers. The most important thing is that you're protected, just in case."

Rianna dropped his hand, then stood and looked down at him. "Just in case? Who or what do I have to fear?"

"Rianna, sit down. I'm doing my best to say this as straight as I know it."

She sat. Barely.

"Relax," he said. "Trust me."

"I'll relax when you start speaking bluntly."

He sat back and threw up his hands. "Okay. I have a man tracking the homicide investigation in San Francisco and working his own leads on Al's case. If enough evidence turns up to prove that low-life drug dealer took his revenge for doing five years in the state pen, I'll know it before the police do. If revenge was the motive, you have nothing to fear."

"What if it's not?"

"Until we hear either way, you need to be protected."

"What you're not saying," Rianna stated slowly, "is that if the drug dealer didn't do it and something in one of my slides or sketches happens to be incriminating evidence against someone, I might end up like Al."

Ty took her hand into his own. "Not if I'm around twenty-four hours a day. I promise."

"You?"

"Why not? I'm involved in both cases. It makes sense."

"But—you? Twenty-four hours a day?"

Ty grimaced. "Al could have been gunned down at midnight as easily as he was at high noon. And don't forget that you're reckless enough to live in a house with good door and window locks but no alarm system. Anyone with a little know-how could break into this place in a minute at midnight and you wouldn't have a chance."

"You're beginning to sound like my father." Rianna edged away. "If he had his way, I'd ride to the corner grocery in an armored limousine and sleep in a mansion surrounded by guard dogs and laser alarms. I'd never have a normal life."

"Rianna—" Ty tightened his grip on her hand "—being robbed or raped or dying young isn't normal, either. I had an alarm system installed in my condo the day I moved in. It's state-of-the-art and I sleep easy knowing that. Under the circumstances you need someone here around the clock or I won't sleep easy, period."

"Does the someone have to be you?"

"No," he replied with some difficulty. It was no easier to add, "You're free to hire your own man if you want. I can recommend someone. In any event you need someone you can trust with your life."

"Ty, this morning you said you'd only guard me if you had to."

"Yeah. I know I didn't score winning points with you this morning and my only flimsy excuse is this." He touched a finger to the bandage on his forehead and feigned a muddled smile. "I wasn't thinking straight after the fall." *I'm not thinking straight now, either. Holding your hand and breathing in your perfume make me dizzy enough to know I'll never regain my wits if you choose me for your full-time bodyguard. Say you want someone else. Save me from what's beginning to look like a dream come true, and from the day I'll be forced to wake up.*

She reached out her free hand, then pulled back. "I forgot to ask about your stitches," she said with an apologetic catch in her voice. "How many?"

"Four."

"Do they hurt?"

"No, not really. How do I look in a bandage? Ridiculous?"

"No. Rakish."

He smiled at that. Rianna smiled back and looked into his eyes, still struck by the passion and conviction he'd displayed when he told her about his work to save endangered animals. A man with their best interests at heart would be as trustworthy and staunch a defense as any endangered human being could have. A man who was turning out to be such a temptation, however, would be an even greater one as a full-time bodyguard.

She averted her eyes and looked down at her hand in his. Tiny streams of sensation radiated up her arm from the heat of his fingers on her skin. With his merest touch making a high-voltage conductor of her hand, what would a prolonged acquaintance with him do to the rest of her?

Though falling into bed with Ty might prove unavoidable and well worth any subsequent regrets, falling in love with him would be disaster. Nathan Breece could abide many men, but never a Tyler Toranaga.

With great effort she pulled her hand free of Ty's and said in a cooler tone, "There was a moment this morning when you appeared to hate me."

"Not you." Ty stood up and jammed his fists into his pockets. "It pushed one of my Hot buttons when you thought I'd been hired by your father. I hated the idea of that."

"Why?"

"Read his newspapers sometime."

"I do, along with several others."

"And you agree with the bias he puts on the news?"

"Ty, a lot of people, including me, don't agree with every word he prints. On the other hand a lot of people do."

"I'm not one of them."

"That's the whole idea, isn't it? Freedom of the press guarantees that we all have a choice in what we can print and read in this country," she countered.

He waved a hand in dismissal. "We could argue your father's narrow-minded editorials all night and never agree. What's important right now isn't his opinions or anyone's constitutional right to a free press. Do you want me to protect you or not?"

"I'm not sure. I have bad memories of the time my father hired bodyguards for my mother and me after Patty Hearst was kidnapped and held for ransom. I was an only child and I hated being crowded and confined. There was always someone on the other side of every door or in the seat behind me, always someone listening on the phone extension. But then you already know that about me, don't you?"

Ty sat down again, but kept his distance. "I do my homework," he acknowledged and added, "Look, it's no picnic to have someone breathing down your neck day and night, but it's no pleasure cruise to be a sitting duck, either."

"If only this house weren't so small, with only one bedroom and bath," she lamented. "My office is too cramped to squeeze a cot in...though this sofa does fold out into a double bed."

"I've slept in my share of tight spots." Ty propped one foot on the coffee table. "I won't be here forever, you know."

Rianna gave him a long, direct look. "You'd have a gun handy most of the time, I suppose."

"Within reach."

"Where is it now?"

"Within reach."

"You aren't a man of your word. I hate guns."

"Al's murderer doesn't."

She slumped back into the cushions. "Why me? Why you?"

"God knows."

Quelling the strongest urge he'd ever had to take a woman into his arms and kiss her into acquiescence, Ty stared at the stained-glass window on the wall directly across from him. Rainbows. Romance. Rianna. Here were risks he should never consider taking. Never.

It seemed forever before she spoke. "When would you want to start?"

"Right now."

4

A MAN IN THE HOUSE.

Riveted by that thought, Rianna stared at the opening sentence of the romantic suspense novel she had been attempting to read for thirty minutes. Any other sleepless night would have found her well beyond the first chapter in that half hour. Not tonight.

A man. Several hours ago she had feared him. Now Tyler Toranaga slept just feet away on the other side of her bedroom door. Asleep in her sofa bed. With his loaded automatic revolver under his pillow.

Rianna trembled. The gun was the cause of her tremor. Blaming cold gunmetal was preferable to admitting that the real reason was Ty.

Resolved not to focus again on him, she tackled the first word of the first sentence of the first chapter again. Word by word she made her laborious way to the first period—and found once again that she hadn't comprehended even the first syllable.

Rianna gave up and closed the book. She glanced at her bedroom door. At Ty's insistence, it had been left slightly open. But his presence on the other side was too potent a force to be ignored. After all, he wasn't any man. He was the man who made her heart skip each time his eyes met hers, who with his first touch had set off a restless yearning inside her.

She thought back to the moment at Casanova when the look on Ty's face had led her to envision his lips pressed hotly, hungrily on hers. Had she misinterpreted his expression? Perhaps. But there was no doubt in her mind that he had thought about kissing her since then. She had caught him gazing at her too many times to doubt it. Had their evening together been a date, it would have ended with more than one good-night kiss.

Closing her eyes, Rianna imagined Ty gathering her into his muscled arms, fusing his seductive mouth with hers. Rianna and Ty, Ty and Rianna . . .

If only their first names were all that mattered. Knowing they weren't, she forced her eyes open. It was dangerous as well as foolish to think no further than first names. Breece and Toranaga. Oil and water. Unfortunately the reminder wasn't strong enough to keep Ty's image from dominating her thoughts even after she snapped out her bedside lamp.

Wide-eyed at his own imaginings, Ty saw the wedge of light go dark. For the twentieth time since he had slipped between the sheets, he punched his pillow into submission. Earlier, in mutual, discomfited silence, he and Rianna had made up the sofa bed. Never again, he vowed, would he make a bed with Rianna Breece's assistance unless she intended to join him in it. He couldn't forget how her slim, deft hands had smoothed over half of the fabric that now touched his skin. Equal torture came with the memory of her shapely breasts curving and shifting against the silk bodice of her dress as she tucked sheet corners tight and coaxed pillows into cases.

He wanted her.

Scowling into the darkness, Ty clasped his hands behind his head. The only woman he shouldn't want, he wanted. He got hard just thinking about it. Worse, he'd walked straight into the situation with his eyes wide open as they were right now. How many nights could he lie like this, a room apart from Rianna Breece?

On the opposite side of the bedroom door, Rianna stared into the darkness. There was no deeper, darker pit than insomnia. Some toss-and-turn nights were worse than others, and tonight ranked right up there with the worst. On occasions like this she usually ended up in her studio, sketching, framing, cleaning brushes. But this time there was a man in the house.

That fact alone was enough to inhibit another habit or two, such as her preference for sleeping in the nude. She was wearing her only pair of pajamas, and they were not only uncomfortable, but irritating. Almost as irritating as lying in bed wide-awake while the rest of the world slept. Rianna tossed and turned in mounting discomfort. Her pajama top felt like a straitjacket. Her ears rang in the silent darkness. Her eyes would *not* stay shut. She sat up in sudden rebellion. So what if Ty slept in the next room? Whose house was it, anyway?

She got out of bed and tied a fuchsia silk robe over her pink flannel pajamas. An hour or two at the easel painting Squeeze's innumerable scales should beckon the sandman. The real trick, however, would be to slip past the strongman in the next room without waking him.

Ty heard each move Rianna made—from the faint squeak of the hinge as she tiptoed through the doorway, to the whisper of silk on flannel, and the intake and outflow of her breathing—in the silent room. With each of her tentative steps the scent of her perfume floated closer. He waited motionless until her fragrance surrounded him and her body heat warmed the air.

Rianna tensed and paused. Just a few more steps and she'd be past him. *Some bodyguard,* she thought with a pang of disappointment. He was so deeply asleep, she couldn't even hear him breathe. She recalled that Brent had slept like that. Dead to the world. Like a man with a clear conscience. Did he still sleep soundly? She realized that she no longer cared. She was indifferent toward Brent. Finally. What a strange, welcome sensation!

What she felt next was a strong and warm hand grasping her wrist from behind. *Ty!* His grip whirled her halfway around and held her immobile with her arm jackknifed against her lower back. His hold on her almost, but didn't quite, hurt.

"Don't move one muscle!" Tyler rasped into her ear.

There was no question of moving. Drawn taut as a bow, her arm bent and trapped between her back and his bare chest, she could only gasp, "Let go—it's only me!"

He held her firm. "I know it's only you. Do I pass the bodyguard test?"

"T-test . . . ?"

"Do I measure up?"

Rianna gulped. "I'm only here because I couldn't sleep. I—" She broke off, knowing it wasn't just the shock of Ty's ambush that made speech so difficult. Equally effective was the muscled reality of Ty's chest pressed to her back in the dark, his breath prickling the skin at the curve of her neck, his legs aligned to the backs of her own.

"You aren't testing me?"

"No. I was just—"

His grip loosened slightly. "You should be. How else can you be certain you can trust your life to me?"

"I'm certain now," she shakily assured him.

His clasp on her wrist softened almost to a caress; gently he unfolded her arm and turned her to face him.

He flicked on the standing lamp and studied her face, guiltily noting the pallor in her cheeks and the panic in her eyes. "Hey, I'm sorry I spooked you. I thought . . . I mean . . ."

Rianna's knees suddenly buckled in delayed reaction to being seized by a man in the dark. A man, she could see now, who slept in boxer shorts and nothing else. *Black silk* boxers, if she wasn't mistaken. Further shaken as she recalled how the front of the superb male body wearing those boxers had molded itself to her back, she sank onto the sofa bed.

"Rianna...I'd never, ever..." Ty flicked off the lamp. A moment later he was beside Rianna, cradling her in his arms, whispering his promise that she had nothing to fear as long as he was there.

There was nothing wild in that promise, but wild blood raced through his veins as he made it. Although he couldn't see, he could feel how perfectly her head fitted into the crook of his shoulder. Very lightly he brushed a kiss onto her forehead.

"Ty...I didn't come out here to get too close for comfort."

"I wasn't banking on that, either," he murmured against her temple, his self-control gone.

"We shouldn't..."

He felt her breath on his lips and furrowed her curls with his fingers. "No," he agreed in a whisper. "We shouldn't, should we? We should turn the lamp back on."

"Yes," she whispered back, "we should."

"We're not going to, are we?"

"No. We're going to..." Oh, there was nothing but insanity in wanting to kiss a man her father would blacklist on sight. Yet she wanted it more than anything else.

"Yes, we certainly are going to leave the lamp off," Ty murmured, silently cursing the temporary paralysis that kept his arms around her and his fingers from the switch a mere arm's length away. "We've been moving toward this all night."

For the moment, being in his arms seemed sane and logical rather than crazy. Here in the dark Rianna was simply herself, he simply himself. Nothing complicated about it. Here they were just human beings, male and female, intensely attracted to each other, poised on the brink of a kiss.

"Ty..."

"Rianna..." Ty knew he'd regret a slew of things in the morning if he kissed her, not the least of which would be pretending that he'd never damned the name Breece in his life. Thank God Rianna was wearing pajamas and a robe. If he were skin to skin with her, he'd be welcoming the worst of regrets.

He lowered his head and invited regret.

The instant Ty's parted lips sank onto hers, Rianna quivered. She felt his arms tighten around her. The movement flattened her right hand against his chest and she was aroused by the contrast between the smoothness of his flesh and the hard nub of his left nipple.

Ty had no sooner skated the tip of his tongue over the curve of her lower lip than she was fitting her mouth to the shape of his own. His were lips that plucked, sipped, savored, then held hers for a moment before his tongue plunged in.

Rianna knew then that nothing would ever be quite the same again. She had kissed her share of men, but no first embrace had made her dissolve like this in a man's arms. Under her palm she felt Ty's heart speed up. Her own heart accelerated into a matching rhythm, one she could hear in her ears and feel at every pulse point in her body.

Tyler Toranaga. Mr. Right, all right?

Wrong. Wrong. Mr. Wrong, corrected the inner voice from what little was left of her rational mind. *He's Japanese. Remember? Remember?*

Ty was on the verge of easing Rianna onto his pillows, in pursuit of a thorough exploration of her mouth, when the push of her hand against his chest stopped him. Gentle yet persistent, she pushed again. He wasn't certain how to interpret her slight moan when his tongue slid back and his lips released hers. He only knew that he hadn't been alone in wanting to forge ahead to where that kiss had been leading.

He was also sure that a flick of a lamp switch would reveal a flush on Rianna's cheeks, dilated pupils, lips ready to kiss and kiss again. Lamplight would also reveal his own response. Black silk couldn't conceal what soul kissing Rianna Breece in the dark did to a man. He needed darkness to recover, but felt her move away and reach for the lamp.

"No. Not yet." He drew her back.

"We—this shouldn't have happened, Ty. If you're willing to forget it did, so am I." She reached out again.

"Leave it off, Rianna," he commanded softly, gripping her shoulders and holding her still.

"I can't see," she protested, feeling increasingly desperate to escape him and appalled at what she had done. "Stop manhandling me. You have no right."

Ty held her firmly and said tersely, "I'm not claiming any rights where you're concerned."

"What do you think you're doing then?"

"I—"

"If you think I have any intention of letting that happen more than once, you're wrong." She stiffened in anger at the man she had only moments ago felt she could trust and haughtily added, "You're also fired, Mr. Toranaga, if this is the way you handle the bodies you guard."

"I volunteered for this job, Miss Breece, and I am *not* manhandling you. I'm only asking you to leave the blasted lights out until I've spent a minute or two imagining myself in a cold shower. You're the artist here. Get the picture?"

"Yes," she said after a second. "I'm sorry I misunderstood."

"You're forgiven. Take care on your way out."

"Don't worry. I know the way in the dark by heart."

"You'll be in the studio, as usual?"

As usual? "Yes." She knew better than to ask how he knew which lights burned in her cottage during her sleepless nights. The eight-foot stone wall enclosing her backyard had evidently proved no barrier to his surveillance of her.

"Don't unlock any doors while you're up," he cautioned. "And keep every shade in the studio down, okay?"

"I always do at night."

"I know. Just making sure nothing happens that shouldn't happen."

Rianna bit her lip. "About what just *did* happen, I shouldn't have—"

"No one's to blame," Ty cut in gently. "Let's leave it at that. No fault. Fifty-fifty."

"Okay." He loosened his grip on her and she slipped away and made her way to the kitchen doorway, where she paused. "Ty?"

"What?"

"Imagine a cold shower for me, too, while you're at it."

FORTY MINUTES LATER she realized there was no use in trying to paint python scales at midnight when nudes were all she could think about. *Make that singular. Nude.* Ty would be one magnificent nude figure study.

Cursing that image, she stabbed her brush into a jar of murky turpentine, coated the bristles with paint from the palette she held and redoubled her efforts. Damn. Her muddled daubs looked more like gingersnap cookies than reptile scales. Sighing in defeat, she scraped the paint off the canvas. Had Ty called her an artist? He should see her now.

What he'd see was a woman who'd made the discovery that she needed a man in her bed in the worst way. She couldn't delude herself that she didn't—not after what she knew she would always remember as the kiss of a lifetime.

Shaking her head in utter dismay, Rianna abandoned her palette and easel in a search of some other distraction that might elbow Ty out of her head and tire her out enough to sleep.

There were always brushes to be cleaned, she mused, wandering over to the utility sink in the corner. One glance at the contents and she discarded the thought. She needed more than grunt work to occupy her mind right now—something that would require every power of concentration. A challenge that would blot everything else from her mind. She moved to the easel she used for watercolors. What challenge?

Fog, perhaps? Yes, fog was perfect. And watercolor, unlike oil, was a fast medium that allowed for only a few mistakes. She hurried back to the sink.

An hour later she was sitting as dejectedly in front of her watercolor labors as she had in front of Squeeze-Play's portrait. How could she paint fog when what she *really* wanted to recreate was—? She stabbed her brush into her water jar. Sitting back in her chair, she closed her eyes. No, she wouldn't, would *not* lay brush upon paper to paint *him*. No matter how vivid her every image of *him* was in her mind, she wouldn't do it.

Painting any object of interest was an act of overwhelming intimacy for her. Rianna had never created the likeness of any animal on canvas without feeling as if she *was* that animal while she painted it. Bringing the image to life demanded that she identify with the subject. She couldn't risk the involvement that painting Ty would bring. Even a pencil sketch would be a shift in the wrong direction.

Still, her fingers itched to sketch his clean-cut features. She forced her eyes open and, resisting the itch, took up her watercolor brush again to paint ethereal fog.

"Would a walk on the beach help?" Ty inquired behind her.

Rianna twisted around in her chair. *Damn him and his stealth.* Taken by surprise for the second time, her heart again slammed against her ribs. "Could you spare a warning knock the next time?" she said as icily as she could.

"I *did* knock," he asserted mildly. "Twice." He walked in. "You seemed to be in a trance."

Almost as unsteadied by the sight of Ty in his black trousers and unbuttoned white dress shirt as she had been by him in skin and black silk, she turned back to stare at her mottled fogscape. *Damn him twice.* Didn't he own a single stitch of clothing that looked only so-so on him rather than spectacular? Even the gauze square taped to his forehead failed to detract from the overall impression. She dunked her brush once more, tapped it against the jar to shake off the water, then dunked it a third time.

It wasn't necessary for her to look around to know that Ty was standing unnervingly close. She felt his presence as he examined the watercolor over her shoulder.

"Nice," he murmured. "Reminds me of this morning when we ran."

Rianna shook her head. With two strokes she slashed a broad black *X* on the painting, making her opinion of it quite clear. She got up, as eager to escape his nearness as to flee the sight of her failure. Now was the time to clean brushes.

"Pretty hard on yourself, aren't you?" said Ty, tracing his index fingertip along one glistening cross stroke of Rianna's black *X*. "Lesser work than this hangs in fine art galleries all over Carmel."

"Nothing with my name on it hangs anywhere unless I'm satisfied with it first," Rianna replied from the sink. "I can do much better than that, when I'm really inspired."

"What really inspires you?"

She rinsed the splayed bristles of a fan brush, wondering if Ty knew the answer to his own question. He hadn't been anything but honest with her since he'd blown his cover. He might be aware that she was still rattled by that kiss, but wouldn't taunt her with it. He'd already shown himself to be too much of a gentleman for that.

Flicking a glance at him over her shoulder, she dryly replied, "Inspiration might strike after a good night's sleep—if I could get it."

"Like I said, a walk on the beach might do it. I could use one, too."

While Rianna considered that tempting proposition, she shaped and smoothed the silky brush against her palm, the same palm she had earlier pressed so fervently to Ty's chest. A spot of heat blossomed in the center of her hand, accompanied by a flush to her cheeks as she recalled touching him. She ran cold water onto her hand to quench the sensation. It had nearly disappeared when Ty reached around her and rinsed his paint-blackened fingertip under the running water.

"Not tonight," she said, deciding against a walk on the beach with him at her side. Quickly she stepped aside.

His step back matched hers for speed. "Let me know if you change your mind." He wiped his finger on his shirt, chagrined that he had once again lost control of his senses.

He couldn't remember ever being so vulnerable to a woman's proximity. Had she been wearing a sexy negligee, he could have said he'd simply been provoked. Provocative, however, was not a word to describe pink flannel from neck to toe with fuchsia silk swathed over it. Yet Rianna might have been wearing peekaboo lace and black garters for all the self-possession he could claim in her presence.

The time spent imagining himself in an arctic shower had been followed by a rush of regret at having kissed her, then by even greater regret that he'd only kissed her once.

Ty needed to get as far away from her as he could, so he moved to the far end of the studio where a long table stood stacked with boxes of photographic slides, art supplies and sketches. Among the boxes he saw a pottery mug half-emptied of coffee and a Big Mac carton that had been used as an ashtray. Ty homed in for a closer look at its contents. "Is this your cheroot?"

"What's a cheroot?" Rianna asked without turning from the sink."

"A cigar." Ty picked up the carton. "I take it this isn't yours?"

Rianna glanced over her shoulder. "Oh, that's Mr. Bernson's." She wrinkled her nose and went on with her task. "He brought his own lunch and smoked like a chimney while he was here, as you can see. Nice man otherwise." Engrossed in scraping paint off a brush handle, she was startled to find Ty at her side with the hamburger carton in his hand.

"What was his full name?" he asked.

"Randall Bernson. He—"

Ty cut her off with an urgent grip on her upper arm. "How tall was he?"

"Medium height."

"Build?"

"Stocky."

"Hair?"

"Light brown . . . what there was of it. Sort of wispy on top, fuller on the sides."

"Gray eyes? Wire-rimmed glasses? Age forty-five or so?"

"You know him?"

"Knew him," said Ty. His fingers dug into her arm. "When was he here?"

"About a week ago. He called about having a portrait done of his pet ocelot and arranged to come in the next day and see my work. I showed him a lot of sketches, photos and slides."

"Was he ever alone in here?"

Rianna thought back. "Chloe phoned while he was here. I took the call on the kitchen phone and talked for several minutes."

"Have you noticed anything missing since he was here?"

"Well, no. It never occurred to me to check. I haven't even done any housekeeping in here since then, as you can see."

"Ten to one something's missing," Ty said grimly, releasing her arm. "Can you show me everything you showed him? Every single thing?"

"Sure, but . . . why?"

"Because Bernson wasn't who he said he was."

"Who was he?"

Ty drew a deep breath. "Al. Your description fits. This cigar's his brand, chewed at the end exactly the way he chewed them." He looked down at the stub of the cheroot and shut his eyes for a moment. "Dammit to hell," he swore between gritted teeth. "I told him he'd dig himself an early grave smoking those things. Not that it stopped him. Nothing stopped him until . . ."

His shoulders heaved and Rianna pulled out a stool, urging Ty onto it. Seated, he propped one elbow on the table and covered his eyes with his hand.

Rianna pulled up a stool next to him and curved her arm around his shoulders. "I know, Ty. . . . I know. . . . It's never easy," she murmured.

Her mother had committed suicide several years ago, so she did know how helpless and grief-stricken the sudden death of a loved one could leave those who lived on. Not only was Ty's grief fresh, but he hadn't had time to deal with it. She herself was having trouble in dealing with the fact that the pleasant man who had visited her studio the week before would never chomp a cheroot again.

"You'd think an ex-cop would be immune to it, wouldn't you?" Ty muttered, pinching the bridge of his nose hard.

"You cared about him. There's no shame in that, Ty," Rianna said gently, tears filling her eyes.

Rianna had never stopped missing her mother; she still hungered for the mother love that Thea's gunshot wound had cheated her of in her early teens, and suddenly her tears overflowed.

Ty turned and pulled her close. "Why?" he croaked. "Why?"

In one convulsive move they were in each other's arms, both shedding bitter tears at the question that had no answer. Long minutes passed before their weeping subsided. Spent, they held each other in silence before Ty pulled slightly away to look at Rianna.

"I've . . . I haven't let go like that since I was a kid." He wiped his shirt sleeve over his eyes and shook his head. "Phew. You okay?"

Rianna nodded and gave him a weak smile. "It helped to have company. I've always cried alone before."

Ty passed the pad of his thumb over her wet cheek. "I can't imagine why. You look as beautiful in tears as you did in diamonds at dinner."

"You're the one to be complimented," she demurred in a shaky whisper. "It's good to know that real men *do* cry."

Ty shifted his eyes to focus somewhere over her shoulder. "I never saw him shed a tear, but I can tell you Al was a real man. I wish you could have known him better."

"Tell me about him."

His eyes came back to her, clouded again. "Later. After I look through the stuff you showed him. I'm pretty sure he bagged some evidence while you were on the phone that day."

"It couldn't have been anything very big," Rianna reasoned. "He didn't have anything bigger than a briefcase with him."

Ty didn't seem to be listening. Once again he was gazing sympathetically into her eyes.

"You were crying for your mother, weren't you?"

Surprised at his perception, she nodded. With most people she found it impossible to talk about her mother, so Rianna was shocked at how easy it was to speak about her mother with Ty. "She was a great beauty—and a manic-depressive. If she hadn't been reared from day one to take her mother's place as the queen of San Francisco society, she'd have been an artist, too. During the times when she was well, we painted together. She was so talented. I loved her very much."

"Still do and always will."

"Always," Rianna agreed. "For a long time after her death I didn't understand that it was her depressions that killed her. If a gun hadn't been available to her, she might still be..." She sighed. "I don't know why I'm telling you this. It was all headline news in its day. You've read all about it, I'm sure."

Ty tensed the arm he had kept curled around Rianna. "I've never read anything about you hating guns, but I can see you have good reason."

After a wary moment Rianna said, "I have better reason to hate them than anyone but my father knows. You see I..."

Ty felt her shoulders stiffen. He waited, watching her dark lashes sweep down, and noted her hesitation.

"Why am I telling you what I've never told anyone else in the world?" she said.

"Rianna, if you're trusting me with your life, you can trust me with everything else. I'm trusting *you* to keep to yourself how your invincible bodyguard blubbered on your shoulder like a two-year-old tonight."

"A two-year-old! I'm honored that you shared your grief with me," she protested.

"*I'll* feel honored by whatever you want to tell me, then. What is it?"

Rianna bit her lip again. "Remember how the papers reported that my father discovered her and was so distraught that he didn't call the police for almost an hour afterward?"

"Yes."

"He didn't find her, Ty. I did." She closed her eyes tightly and waited for the sorrow she always felt when she let herself remember the pearl-handled revolver in her mother's hand. The sorrow came, but the solid strength of Ty's arm around her blunted the pain—for the first time since her mother's death.

"Good God!" Ty's other arm came around her fast and he rocked her against his chest. "No wonder you're terrified of guns! I'll keep mine out of sight as much as possible," he soothed. "I promise."

Rianna let herself be soothed, let his strength rock away the pain until there was nothing left. Her hand rested on Ty's bare skin where his unbuttoned shirt lay open. From what moment, she asked herself, had she begun to trust Tyler Toranaga so implicitly that she'd been able to confide a secret that only she and her father had shared all these years?

As Ty rocked Rianna, he thought of Nathan Breece shielding his daughter from the lurid publicity. It must have been hell enough for him to endure it, without having to fear that she would be subjected to its mercilessness. Then there was the knowledge that he couldn't protect her from the trauma of what she had witnessed. What little sympathy Ty could spare for Rianna's father, he spared now. He wouldn't wish a tragedy like that on anybody.

Nor did he wish himself at that moment anywhere but right where he was, with Rianna in his arms. If anything, he wished he could hold her to himself forever and damn every reason he shouldn't! He couldn't forget that she had experienced enough grief to mingle her tears with his own. The emotional bond that they had just forged was even more intimate—in its own way—than the kiss they had shared.

"Ty?"

"Hmm?"

"Thank you for listening to me."

"Thank *you* for a shoulder when I needed one."

"Anytime." *Pull out of his arms right now, or you'll never be able to leave,* Rianna warned herself. Never had so many muscles in her body felt so disinclined to follow orders. With an effort she raised her head from his shoulder. His enticing mouth was inches away. If she wanted to . . .

Instead she said, "Do you want to see the photos, the slides or the sketches first?"

"Uh. . .slides first." Ty was conscious that he should have moved a lot faster to remove himself from temptation. Rianna seemed to be similarly afflicted.

It took them several seconds to come apart and several more before Rianna could recall exactly which box of slides Al had examined.

"Here. Start with these." She handed Ty the box and a slide viewer, then searched through a file cabinet for the photos she had shown Al. She placed the file at Ty's elbow and pointed out the stack of sketches at the other end of the table. "Do you need anything else?"

Ty inserted the first slide into the viewer with unsteady hands. "No, this'll keep me busy for a while." He risked a glance at her across the table. She looked beautiful, vulnerable and so desirable—even in buttoned-to-the-neck pink flannel—that it took everything he had to look into the viewer and say, "I'll close up here when I'm through. You should try to get some sleep."

She nodded and moved in the direction of the door.

Neither the slide in the viewer nor willpower could stop him from watching her walk away. He couldn't tear his eyes away even when she turned in the doorway and met his hungry stare with one that matched it.

"G'night, Ty."

"'Night, Rianna."

NEAR DAWN Ty laid the last set of Kodak prints on the table in front of him and recognized that he'd hit pay dirt.

The storage envelope from the photo store said the prints had been made from a twenty-four-exposure roll of film several months before Al had begun shadowing Rianna. Her notation on the envelope flap, Taken at Quail Haven, meant nothing to Ty. That place-name had never come up in his investigation of animal smuggling.

However the name of the fuzzily focused male face in the background of one of the snow-leopard photos was very familiar. Now Ty held in his hand photographic evidence that linked Crayton Thorn with a rare, endangered animal.

Ty tried to curb his excitement. There was no proof yet that Thorn had smuggled that animal into the country. From circumstantial evidence like this, it was a long way to making charges stick against a wealthy import-export czar. But it was a start. A big start.

Ty sat staring at the photo. How had Al missed this vital piece of evidence? Had Thorn commissioned the snow-leopard portrait? Or had he just been at Quail Haven when Rianna was there and accidentally got caught on film? Had she ever painted the portrait? Who owned Quail Haven and where was it? Too many questions. He needed Rianna.

He was ready to wake her when something about the spread of prints pulled him back. He noticed that the last row was short. There were twenty-two prints where there should have been twenty-four. He checked the envelope and found only negatives. Holding them up to the light, he saw that the last two had been snipped off, but the text on the outside of the envelope said every exposure had been developed and charged for.

That could only mean that Al hadn't missed a thing. Unless Rianna had removed the missing pieces for her own reasons, Al had pocketed two prints and negatives for his files. If he had, his killer now had them.

Ty sighed and rose from his chair, making a mental note to phone his office when it opened and get a lead on Thorn's recent whereabouts. To a paroled drug lord the prints would mean zilch. To Crayton Thorn they'd mean a lot. Ty flipped off the studio lights on his way to her room.

He stopped just short of knocking on her half-open door, asking himself what the hell he thought he was doing. How could he wake a woman who suffered from insomnia to answer his questions, even if they were urgent? They could wait until breakfast, couldn't they? Facing her door, he shoved his hands into his pockets and glanced over his shoulder.

The first vague light of dawn had filtered in around the drawn curtains of the living room, making the shape of his bed visible. He hung his head and stared at his bare feet, recalling how close he and Rianna had earlier come to losing control. Given that, barging into her room and waking her up right now would be one bad idea. He'd be wanting to kiss her before he got his first question out. More than wanting, he'd be *doing* it before she had her eyes half-open.

"Ty. . . is that you?"

He gulped guiltily and took a step back. "Yeah. How come you're not getting some sleep?"

"I did. I woke up a few minutes ago." Rianna sat up and turned on her bedside lamp. "Do you need something?"

She could only see half of him through the door—one bare foot, one dark trouser leg with a fist jammed into the pocket, one half of an unbuttoned white shirt with the sleeve rolled halfway up the muscled forearm.

She didn't have to see his expression to confirm that he wanted what she did—which wasn't solitude in bed.

"Would a walk on the beach help?" she asked.

"That," he said, "would help more than you know."

Rianna swung out of bed. "I *do* know. Let's go."

5

THE WIND at their backs, Rianna and Ty walked silently along the tide line of Carmel Beach. Sea gulls dipped and soared in the gusts above the breakers.

Under his black suit jacket Ty wore an oversize yellow sweatshirt Rianna had loaned him. For warmth, she had dressed in jeans, a navy pullover and a long Irish knit coat sweater.

"Does the name Crayton Thorn ring a bell with you?" Ty asked, breaking the silence during which Rianna and he had greeted the new day.

"No. Should it?" Rianna asked bewildered.

"Maybe. He's in the background of a snow-leopard photo you took a few months ago at Quail Haven, wherever that is."

"Quail Haven. Yes, that's a big ranch back in the wilds of Carmel Valley. And I mean wild enough that I had to borrow Gordo's Jeep to get up there in one piece." She thought for a moment. "I can't say I remember anyone named Crayton Thorn there."

"Who owns the place?"

"A widow. Mrs. Benton."

"Is the leopard hers?"

"She told me it had belonged to her husband. He died last year and provided in his will for a portrait of it to be painted, by me if possible, as a special gift for their only grandchild."

"Did you paint it?"

"Yes. Mrs. Benton was quite pleased. So was I."

"But you don't remember a Crayton Thorn there the day you snapped the pictures?"

Rianna tried to think back. "There were a lot of people there that day for a party she was giving. She didn't introduce me to any of them—or invite me into the crowd. Who's Crayton Thorn?"

"An import-export czar with a shady reputation. Rumors I've heard have led me to suspect he might be involved in smuggling in rare birds and reptiles from South and Central America."

"You think he smuggled the Benton's leopard in?"

"I'm not sure what to think yet. Did Mrs. Benton explain how her husband came to own such a rare animal?"

"She said he bought it from a zoo that sold it because it was sterile."

"Did she say which zoo?"

"Not that I recall. But she did tell me about a national zoo breeding program that's designed to keep the species alive. I just assumed Karima was from one of those zoos. She was a prime animal, just beautiful."

"Any other animals there?"

"Several. Llamas, two zebras, kangaroos, peacocks everywhere on the grounds, caged birds of every description throughout the house."

"Any parrots, macaws?"

"Both. And others I couldn't even identify. Mr. Benton had acquired quite a menagerie, but nothing in it was as exotic as Karima."

"Would you say Quail Haven is a big-bucks place?"

"Three to four million if it went on the market right now."

"That big." Ty looked pensively out to sea. "You would know, wouldn't you?"

Rianna stiffened and halted in her stride. "What do you mean by that?"

"Just that you know the ins and outs of wealth and privilege better than I do. It's nothing to get touchy about."

"Nothing for *you* to get touchy about, you mean. I know all the ins and outs, but I wasn't born rich by personal request any more than you were born Japanese by request. It's not as if you or I had a choice in either matter, is it?"

"You're the one whose parents had choices mine never dreamed of," Ty asserted, looking up to follow a gull in flight. "That bird up there is freer right now than my parents were for the longest two years of their lives."

"What are you talking about, Ty?"

"Do you know what day this is, Rianna Whitney Breece? It's the anniversary of the day my parents and grandparents were rounded up and relocated during World War II." He turned and started walking with the wind again.

Rianna caught up with him and tugged at his coat sleeve. "Ty. . . I didn't know. I'm sorry."

"I'd like to hear your father and his father say that about the Dirty Jap editorials they ran for years. I don't know who was worse, Nathan Senior during the war or Nathan Junior after it."

"They both had a blind spot after Pearl Harbor. Where were they sent, your family?"

"To Manzanar down in Southern California. They lost their strawberry farm and everything else they'd worked so hard for. My older sister was born there—in a *prison* camp. My grandfather died there of a stroke."

"Again, I'm sorry that happened, Ty."

"Your father isn't."

"That was such a long time ago." Rianna sighed. She slipped her hand into the rigid crook of his elbow and felt the tension ease at her touch. "Some of the wrongs have been righted since then. The government has made financial reparation to former internees."

"A major news story your father's papers managed to bury when Congress passed the redress bill," Ty rejoined. "The U.S. government can make a formal apology, but Nathan Breece can't."

"No, even after all this time he can't," Rianna granted with an apologetic shake of her head. "Losing Uncle Ned at Pearl Harbor was a blow he never recovered from. Like Grandfather before him, Father and his papers will defend the wartime internment of Japanese-Americans until the day he dies."

Arm in arm now, they strolled on in a renewed silence under the rising sun. Several minutes passed before Ty glanced again at Rianna.

"Aside from being just as hot under the collar at me as I am at you, are you warm enough?"

Rianna nodded in agreement. No sooner had he smiled apologetically at her than she smiled back. A moment later, his arm found its way around her shoulders and hers slid about his waist beneath his jacket.

"Why are you so damned hard to stay mad at for more than a minute?" he murmured.

"I'm wondering the same thing about you."

"Great. We're both in the same fix. Has it occurred to you that the better we get to know each other, the harder it's going to be?"

"That's one argument against any greater familiarity," Rianna reasoned, "unless we can count on ours breeding contempt."

"I have my doubts after last night." Ty checked the urge to rub his cheek against her blond hair. "Contempt was the last thing I felt then. I can just imagine what your father would say if he knew."

"He'd certainly want to relocate my bodyguard out of my living room."

"*You* can still relocate me with a word, Rianna. You want a different bodyguard, I'll call one of my men to come down."

"How could I want any other when Biff Gallagher swears you're the best?"

Ty raised his eyebrows. "Biff doesn't know we're attracted to each other. Or am I only speaking for myself?"

"I think the man who had to conjure up a cold shower for two last night can answer that question himself."

"That's why I say it's not going to be easy from here on in," Ty asserted. "We can say it will, but talk is easy."

"If we stick to talking, Ty, we'll stay out of trouble."

Ty's nod of agreement was rueful as he growled, "Tell that to our hormones. Then tell me I can buy you breakfast as soon as we're back in our shoes. I'm starving."

BY THE TIME they were served coffee and orange juice in the sunny garden courtyard of Ty's favorite breakfast spot, Rianna had learned more about his family background. Familiarity, both in Ty's case and her own, would only lead to further involvement. It would have been better in the long run for her to still her curiosity about him. Yet she couldn't.

Though he had been born years after the release of internees from Manzanar, he shared his parents' lingering hurt and shame. He'd also shared in their struggle to buy back the strawberry farm they'd lost to the mortgage company. He had worked hard in the berry fields and hothouses to put himself through college. And his deceased grandmother Mitsuye held a very special place in his heart.

"Strange that you have a houseful of rainbows," Ty mused over a second cup of coffee. "My grandmother said it was rainbows in the spring at Manzanar that gave her hope that she and her family would one day be treated like the patriotic Americans they were. She had this little rainbow proverb she repeated over and over to me when I was a kid until she had me believing it."

"What was it?"

He stared into his coffee. "You'll think it's hokey."

"No hokier than the five rainbows in my living room, plus the two in my bedroom, I'll bet. Tell me."

"If I do, don't laugh."

"I won't. Besides, I owe you one. You didn't snicker at my walls last night like every other man has."

"How could I, after my grandmother told me a million times that wishes on rainbows are wishes come true?"

Rianna had to clear her throat before she could say, "That's lovely, Ty. Do you still believe she was right?"

"The kid in me likes to think she was. The ex-cop in me knows better."

"What about the man in you?"

"He never forgets the other proverb about being careful what one wishes, because one might get it." Ty looked at Rianna with a boyish smile. "What does the kid in you think?"

"She likes to think Mitsuye was right, too."

"And the woman in you?"

"She hasn't believed in wishes come true since Brent left her standing at the altar. She also thinks she should change the subject at this point."

"From Brent Halston to what?"

"To something safe and impersonal."

"I'm sorry he did that to you, Rianna. I know how it feels to be dumped. My ex couldn't take being a cop's wife. When she left me for an accountant who worked a steady nine to five and came home for dinner every night, we were already on the rocks. But it gouged me just the same. What happened to you was—"

"What happened to me," she broke in, "was top story for every newspaper and newscast in this country. Try reading lies about yourself in the supermarket tabloids if you want to feel really gouged."

Ty gave her a long, level look before he said, "I've had a lie or two written about me. We have more in common than you think." Seeing her puzzled expression, he added, "It happened that summer you spent in Kenya, and I don't want to talk about it right now any more than you want to talk about getting jilted by a jerk."

"Ty, what . . . ?"

He shook his head and studied his menu. "What are you going to order?"

"The Greek omelet, if our waiter ever comes back," Rianna replied, curious about Ty's cryptic statement, but relieved to escape further discussion of her aborted wedding. "What are *you* having?"

"The Tex-Mex omelet with guacamole." Ty looked around for the waiter. "I imagine he's taking his time because he assumes we're honeymooners with hours to fritter away on breakfast, beach and bed, like everyone else here. How's that for a change of subject?"

"Not bad, but everyone else here is drinking champagne in their orange juice and admiring their shiny new rings. We aren't."

"Maybe he just assumes we're madly in love, then."

"If he does, he isn't very observant."

"I am," Ty said,leaning forward to cover her hand with his. "To really change the subject, you look radiant right now. It's hard to believe you only had a few hours' sleep."

"Ty. . ." She felt the morning sun warm on her back, Ty's thumb, even warmer, rubbing back and forth over her knuckles. She tried again, and this time her voice shook. "Ty. . . this isn't . . . we aren't . . ."

"Halston was a fool to let you go," Ty told her. "How could money matter to him more than you did?"

She bit her lip. "The answer is that money was all for him. He hid it well until Wall Street crashed. When his French countess's father didn't insist on a premarital financial agreement like mine had, he went French."

"Greedy coward." Ty seethed.

"You sound like Father."

"For the first and last time in my life, I hope. I'm not overjoyed to share even that excellent opinion with him."

"He has his faults and blind spots, Ty, but I love and respect him for being the best father he could be to me. Surely you can understand that."

Ty turned her hand over and stroked her palm as he'd stroked her knuckles. "I know you do. What I don't know—unless you feel like telling me—is whether you're carrying a torch for Halston."

"No. I'm not."

Their waiter returned and beamed at the sight of their joined hands. "What, no wedding bands to show off?" he inquired.

"Not yet," said Ty with a secret smile for Rianna. "We're working on it, aren't we, Rainbow?"

"Rainbow. What a beautiful name. Well now—" the waiter poised his pen "—what would the most beautiful couple in the place like to work on for breakfast?"

"Hey, he believed every word of it," Ty commented with a laugh after their orders had been taken and their coffee cups refilled.

Rianna inched her hand out of his. "Really, Ty. Rainbow. Only in California. And why let the poor man think we're headed for the altar any day now?"

"Why not? You don't know him, do you?"

"No. In Carmel waiters come and go like ocean tides."

"So what's the harm in putting him on?"

"What's the point? We aren't in love. Why pretend?"

Ty considered that as he savored a sip of coffee, then replied, "Maybe I want to fall in love just a little, Rainbow."

Something was happening here, she warned herself. Given half a chance, it showed every sign of mushrooming into a matter of the heart.

"Maybe you live dangerously on a daily basis, Ty, but I don't."

"What if I don't live a dangerous emotional life on a daily basis? What if I haven't been involved with a woman for years?" Ty knew he shouldn't pursue this line of questioning, yet couldn't pull back. Somewhere between sundown and sunup he'd stepped into dangerous territory. Now the only question was how far he could afford to go. He wasn't prepared to turn back.

Rianna gave him a frank, measuring look. "Are you trying to seduce me?"

"No, seduction isn't my style. I'm just laying my cards out on the table in case something happens."

"Nothing's going to happen if we keep busy," Rianna replied, her tone brisk and decisive.

"What do you have planned to keep things at the status quo?"

"A lot. We have a lot to do today. We still have to stop by your hotel room and pick up a change of clothes. Are you sure you don't want to check out?"

"Yep. No one who might be interested should get the bright idea that I'm living with you. We'll—er, *I'll* mess up the bed and steam up the bathroom at the hotel to keep things looking normal."

"Okay. After that, we'll go home and clean up and I'll paint until six or seven. While I'm painting, you'll be busy sifting through more slides and sketches. When do your stitches come out, by the way?"

"Couple of days."

"Good. Where shall we have dinner tonight?"

"Whoa. Slow down the agenda. I haven't even bought you breakfast yet."

"How about the West Wind? It's a nice drive down there and the view is spectacular. I'll buy. We'll rent a video on the way back, something wholesome with a PG rating. Then—"

"Are you always this eager to exhaust a man who hasn't had a lick of sleep all night?" Ty interrupted.

"Oh. I forgot," Rianna said sheepishly. "You don't look as if you've missed a wink."

"I'm beginning to feel it, though. Good thing I learned to sleep at will when I was working vice. I'll take a catnap while you paint."

"You can sleep just like that?" She snapped her fingers.

"'Fraid so. Just like that."

"Lucky you. With only two hours on my last sleep log, I'll be dragging all-day."

"If you catch a catnap whenever *I* do," Ty suggested with a wink, "you'll catch up."

A catnap with Ty. An image sprang to life in her head—one so erotic that Rianna had to remind herself that he'd said little to evoke it. He hadn't suggested that she nap *with* him. *When* had been the operative word.

Off-limits! Why couldn't she remember that for more than a half second at a time and repress the sexual warmth she was feeling? When she looked up from stirring her coffee as hard as she could, she found a pained expression on Ty's face.

"I didn't mean that the way it sounded," he muttered. "You're right about keeping busy. If we do, nothing can happen."

Ty only wished he could believe it. The vulnerability in Rianna's eyes prompted him to vow that he wouldn't push any faster than she was willing to move. But he'd push right up to the word no.

WHILE RIANNA PAINTED the afternoon away, he continued browsing through slides of her paintings. The more he studied them, the more intrigued he became. How much of herself she put into her work!

Only a shy woman could have captured that sidelong look in a zoo gorilla's eye, wanting to trust yet not quite sure. The great ape looked ready to bolt even as it stretched out a finger to touch. In another pose, the gentle giant sat tense and still. Rianna was so skilled that Ty could sense how the animal had retreated into its own inner world.

He was reminded of Rianna on her wedding day—how she had faced the invading lenses of press and TV cameras. As silent and impermeable as an animal on display, she had withdrawn herself. Ty realized now what that had cost her.

As he worked his way through the slides, he recognized that there dwelled a depth of emotion in each painting, one that evoked corresponding feelings in himself. Joy, heartbreak, fear, triumph, love were what he saw and felt in the eyes, expressions and body language Rianna had captured in images of animals as diverse as mutts and musk-oxen.

Several times that afternoon he looked up from the slide viewer to catch a glimpse of her, sitting at her easel painting a python. In those surreptitious moments, Ty fantasized about Rianna.

How easy it would be to nuzzle a kiss upon the delicate flesh below her ear! How easy to slip his hands around her from behind and cup her breasts in his palms, feel her nipples bud in response to his fingertips!

Each time the fantasy grew too hard to bear, he retreated to the living-room sofa for a short catnap that calmed his body and cleaned his mind. In the late afternoon he woke to find Rianna standing in the kitchen doorway, looking at him.

"Would you like clam chowder for lunch?" she asked, almost a full minute after his eyes opened and locked with hers. The chowder and two more catnaps tided him over until dinner.

RIANNA WAS ADAMANT that her red Subaru, not his coupe, would deliver Ty and herself to dinner at the West Wind. "I'm buying. I'm driving," she told him.

Ty didn't argue. He'd already learned in one afternoon that she could be stubbornly independent. He wasn't averse to her chauffeuring him tonight. On the contrary, he welcomed it. It was easier to keep an eye out for anything unusual if you weren't compelled to keep the other eye on the road.

It was also a cinch to be able to glance at Rianna's legs in their sheer black nylons as she shifted gears, heading south on winding Highway 1. She wore a black V-necked sweater, a matching slim skirt and the same diamond stud earrings as the night before.

Ty wondered if she knew that his tongue longed to heat up those icelike chips sunk in the soft lobes of her ears. He wondered how she'd respond if he did, then reflected that he'd find out before long; there was dancing as well as dinner at West Wind. A man could get very personal with a diamond stud during a slow dance.

If he asks you to dance, Rianna told herself on the last highway curve before the restaurant came into view, *politely decline. Then again, maybe he's a disaster on a dance floor and won't ask. You can never tell just by looking at a man whether he can dance or not.* Brent, for instance, who had been able to wear a tuxedo with a savoir faire that even James Bond would have envied, could *not* dance.

She took another look at Ty. He was wearing a conventional navy blazer and fawn slacks with a flair that outclassed Brent. *Can probably out-dirty-dance Patrick Swayze. You'll definitely decline, lady!*

Her resolve to refuse held firm all the way through their mesquite-grilled swordfish dinner, and a discussion of recent movies they had seen.

She and Ty were finishing the last of a bottle of chardonnay when Ty touched the lip of his wineglass to hers.

"Here's to one very special artist," he said. "I'd collect your work in a second if I could afford it. Maybe if I sold my Nordstrom to the highest bidder..."

"Sold it! Don't be foolish, Ty. Nordstrom's work is twice as valuable as mine right now."

Ty shrugged. "All the same, I could be tempted to relinquish *Hope* for the sake of what touched me this afternoon. I know it's hard for you to accept praise, Rainbow. I saw what a perfectionist you are in your work. I saw other things, too...."

Should she tell him about *Hope?* Rianna wondered. No. She shouldn't want him to know, even less want to ask Ty what he had seen in her own work. What else could they talk about?

"What... things?"

"Your love for God's earth and its creatures, for one. It lives in every brush stroke. You really get inside each animal, don't you?"

"You saw that?"

"Immediately. I also saw that you've felt hounded into a corner just as some of those animals have been. Haven't you?"

"Yes."

"That cheetah you painted on the Serengeti—the one yawning against the setting sun. You felt her utter contentment and made it so real that *I* felt it." His lips curved into a slow smile. "It brought on my last catnap, as a matter of fact."

Rianna smiled back, affected by his perceptiveness. She suddenly knew that she'd rarely have to explain herself to Tyler Toranaga.

So when the dance band struck up the first tune of the evening, Rianna couldn't decline a sinuous samba with the private eye who had understood her—with ease and empathy. And just as she had sensed in the car, Ty was no leaden-footed box stepper. He had rhythm to burn.

Three steps into the Brazilian beat, he knew the same about Rianna. He brought his open hand hard against her lower back until her hips and thighs were mated to every move he made.

Rianna melted into him. She was glad the dance floor was packed, with herself and Ty sardined in the middle. The way she was glued to him, cheek to cheek, thigh to thigh, was nothing she wanted anyone else observing too closely. She knew her cheeks were flaming and wondered if he could feel her burn where their faces touched.

"You know..." He pulled back a little. "We're a perfect fit, no matter what we'd like to think otherwise."

"We shouldn't be, but we are. I could do this all night with you, Ty."

"I just happen to have all night, Rianna." Once more he laid his cheek against hers and slid up a hand between her shoulder blades to mold her breasts to the shape of his chest.

"We shouldn't."

"You're the one who suggested all night."

"I . . . meant it, but . . ."

"I know what you meant," he murmured. "You love to dance almost as much as you love to paint."

"You know too much, Ty."

"I know you look too beautiful in black cashmere and diamonds, Rainbow."

Rianna felt his lips brush her temple, then dip to her ear, where they pressed a soft kiss upon the opening. She closed her eyes and felt every beat of her heart repeat the sexual tempo of the samba. Her right hand gripped Ty's guiding left for dear life as his lips opened slightly and his tongue traced a slow circle around the diamond stud in her earlobe.

Ty was blowing lightly upon that moist circle and sending Rianna crazy when they were bumped hard from the side by another couple.

"Rianna darling! That *is* you, isn't it? How perfectly droll to collide like this."

She was jolted out of both Ty's embrace and her sensual daze with dizzying speed at the sound of that familiar voice. There on the arm of yet another blond gigolo stood Gordo's thrice-divorced mother, Marjorie Breece-Davies. A chignoned brunette who had benefited from extensive and expensive plastic surgery, she wore her flamboyant designer silks and gold jewelry with haughty verve.

"Mame, I thought you were in Rome until June," Rianna said, kissing her aunt's unlined cheek.

"Rome." Mame made as much of a grimace as her skintight visage would allow. "So dreary this year. Such *hordes* of uncivilized Americans." She tapped her elegant young man on the arm with a jeweled forefinger and gestured at Rianna. "Giulio Romagnoli, meet my lovely niece, Rianna."

Suave in a silk suit, Giulio kissed Rianna's hand with an indolent air and returned to looking monumentally bored.

"Mame Breece-Davies, Giulio Romagnoli, my—er, friend, Tyler Toranaga."

Mame offered her hand to be kissed, but Ty merely shook it, as he did Giulio's. "Nice to meet you both," he said, aware that Mame's narrow green eyes had been taking his measure and were reflecting her displeasure at what they saw.

The floor began to clear with the end of the samba, and Mame invited, "Join us, darlings, please. We're in that precious nook in the side wing."

Before Rianna could open her mouth, Ty had replied. "Thank you, but I promised Rianna we'd leave after one dance. She has a headache."

"Another time, then." Mame kissed the air on either side of Rianna's cheeks and in a quick whisper inquired, "Slumming, dear?" Just as quickly, she stepped back and waved them away. "Ciao, darlings. See you here and there."

"GIVE ME THE KEYS. I'll drive."

Rianna handed them to him without a word.

"So much for dancing all night," Ty grumbled once they were headed back to Carmel.

"Thanks for saving me with a fake headache."

"You?" Ty snorted. "I was saving myself. One more 'darling' and I'd have gagged. Who was the leech in the thousand-dollar suit that she can't do without his company?"

"One of many, Ty. Too many. When she's no longer amused by one, she scrapes up another—and he's always a blonde like Gordo's philandering father, who left her for an eighteen-year-old before Gordo was born."

"Was she the way she is now, back then?"

"Father says she was born that way."

"In that case, Giulio must be on the way out if she sincerely wanted us to join the two of them in their 'precious nook.'"

Rianna sighed. "He'll be history by next week, I suspect." She stared out the window and scowled. "She never comes back from Rome until June. Why did dear Auntie Mame have to pop up tonight, of all nights?"

"Yeah. Why did she have to come along and save us from ourselves? One more dance with you and I'd have been breaking the speed limit to get you back home and into bed."

Rianna flushed, knowing she'd have been just as eager to reach the same destination. "That's not what I meant. In that sense she did us a favor. What I meant was that Mame's a one-woman grapevine. Now that she's seen us together, she'll spread the word."

Ty was silent for a beat. "How far?"

"Straight to San Francisco."

"How fast?"

"By morning."

"How perfectly droll for dear old Dad darling."

"He'll be furious." Rianna shut her eyes and shook her head. "Just furious."

6

A MAN IN THE HOUSE AGAIN.

And a replay of the night before, replete with frustration and then some. Rianna wore the same pink flannel pajamas. Suffered from the same insomnia. Was reading the same first sentence of the same romantic suspense novel. Loathed knowing that the same gun lay under the pillow of the same bed, where that man slept in heaven only knows what color of silk boxers.

To top it all, she had a phone call from her irate father to look forward to in the morning.

She glanced at the clock. Midnight. She stuck her tongue out at the paperback she held and clapped the book shut. So much for romance and suspense. There was enough of that right now in her living room without reading about it on the side.

A light knock sounded on her bedroom door.

"Rianna?"

Just what she needed. Ty in silk boxers, speaking her name as if it were a one-word love poem.

"What?"

"You okay?"

"Of course."

"A likely story. May I come in?"

"For what?"

"You're keeping me awake, biting your nails in there."

"Who's worrying?"

"Don't kid an ex-cop. If Daddy dearest rang right now, you'd jump out of your skin."

"He'll wait until business hours. He always does. What do you want?"

"I have something that might help you sleep."

Rianna didn't doubt that he had everything she needed. A man who could move on a dance floor like Ty did wouldn't leave a woman in bed sleepless, with unfulfilled desires.

"Ty, I know what you're up to without asking, so I'll be perfectly frank. I don't have sex with strange men just to get a good night's sleep."

"Well, I hope not. I simply thought you'd like a not-so-strange man to read you to sleep for a change."

"Oh." She could feel that her sudden blush was several shades darker than her pajamas.

"How about *Shogun* instead of bedtime stories? I found it in the bookcase out here."

So not only could he move with the stealth of a jungle cat, he could see in the dark, too. Rianna knew she should say no, but after having so embarrassingly misread his motive—if he was telling the truth—she couldn't.

"Uh . . . *Shogun* sounds interesting enough."

He was in the room and walking toward her, shirtless and barefoot, wearing gray sweatpants. She could see from a narrow strip of color above the drawstring of his pants that he wore maroon boxers underneath.

Black, maroon—silky and sexy—he must have a wardrobe of them.

As if it were something he did night after night, he sat down on the empty side of her mattress with his back against the headboard and hauled up his legs next to her. Opening the dog-eared book, he said, "Relax. Lie down. You can't sleep sitting up."

"I'm sitting because I was trying to read *myself* to sleep." She tossed her romance novel onto the floor and slipped under the covers. "There. Is that better?"

"As long as you're comfortable," Ty said mildly. "And stop looking at me like I'm the wolf and you're Red Riding Hood. I'm here to read. That's all." He riffled the pages of the thick paperback in his hand. "Did you buy this used or break it in yourself?"

"It's a favorite," she admitted. "Have *you* read it?"

"Nope. Just saw the TV miniseries when it came out. What's your favorite chapter?"

The one where Blackthorne and Mariko make love. "Start anywhere, but skip the blood and gore parts."

"Okay. No beheadings, no battle scenes."

He began, as luck would have it, just a few pages before the love scene she loved. Rianna closed her eyes.

He read smoothly and with great feeling. More than hearing the author's words, Rianna concentrated on the husky timbre of Ty's voice. So soothing . . .

Relaxing deeper into her pillow with each word, she let his voice lure her far away from the rainbowed walls of her bedroom to the exotic castles of feudal Japan, where shoguns were named Toranaga and every handsome samurai lord looked like the bodyguard on her bed.

Ty marked the exact moment when Rianna's breathing segued from drowsiness into slumber. He read steadily on until Mariko and Blackthorne had attained the "clouds and rain" of sexual ecstasy. Then, certain that Rianna was asleep, he let his voice die away after Blackthorne's declaration of love everlasting.

At that moment, Ty himself felt like making a heartfelt declaration. Rianna was as beautiful and desirable asleep as awake, he thought. For the first time he was seeing her peaceful, relaxed, at rest. He fantasized about waking up next to that lovely face each morning. But after meeting Mame tonight, there was no forgetting who he was, who Rianna was. Falling in love even a little would be a little too much.

He wondered if the lightest of kisses would wake her and feared that it would. Would experiencing the clouds and rain with Rianna be as ecstatic as he'd imagined all day? He knew it would. Certain he'd wake her if he left the bed, he switched off her lamp without a click and slid beneath the down comforter.

RIANNA STIRRED IN BED and rubbed the last of a full night's dreams out of her eyes. She smelled the fragrance of brewing coffee.

She rolled onto her back under the downy warmth of her comforter and lay still, blinking at the sunlight that was pouring in through her bedroom window. She had slept! For hours, it seemed. Closing her eyes again, she let the realization sink in. She had slept like a baby from midnight to midmorning for the first time since her ill-fated wedding day.

Why, she had even dreamed! About what? She tried to remember. About Ty. . . ? A dream of Ty kissing her brow? Yes. Another dream—of curling her spine into the protective curve of Ty's solid body and feeling his hand cupped to her breast? Yes.

Such dreams. Turning onto her side to snuggle back in and savor the memory, she saw that the down pillow next to hers bore the definite imprint of a head and showed every sign of a night's heavy use. She sat up and took in the wrinkled pillowcase, a straight black hair caught on it, the rumpled sheets that were never this mussed when she slept alone. She lifted the pillow to her face and breathed in the faint, musky scent of her bodyguard.

She tracked Ty down in the kitchen. He was still barefoot, still shirtless in gray sweatpants, and happily watering plants when she stormed in.

He looked up and grinned. "Hi. Coffee's on. Want a cup?"

"You slept in my bed!" she accused without preamble.

"I was afraid you'd wake if I moved."

"You cuddled up to me all night in my bed without my permission to do anything but read. God knows what else you did."

"I didn't—"

"That's the last time you read to me in bed, Tyler Toranaga."

Ty's face darkened. "Fine with me, Rianna Breece. Go around every day with circles under your eyes." He went to the sink and noisily refilled the watering can. "I was only trying to help in the only way I could."

Rianna gritted her teeth. "We are *not* supposed to be sleeping together. We both agreed."

"We agreed that nothing would happen and nothing did," he retorted. "If it had, you wouldn't have slept through it, believe me. Calm down."

He set down the watering can with a thud. "What would be so bad if something *did* happen, I'd like to know? It's not as if we wouldn't be as fantastic in bed together as we were on the dance floor last night."

"*That's* exactly what would be so bad," Rianna said, sloshing coffee into a mug for herself. "I don't want to be fantastic in bed with anyone I can't love, you included. Just stay out of my bed from now on, Ty."

"You visited mine before I visited yours, if you'll recall. While you were there, you kissed me like you wanted me in the worst way. Did I come screaming at you first thing in the morning?"

"No, you certainly didn't. Love is never a prerequisite for a man in this world."

"Listen, that's—"

"Don't cop out and say that's life. I don't love that way."

"What makes you think *I* do? I have a few sexual standards of my own."

Rianna rolled her eyes in disbelief.

"Okay," Ty conceded after a tense pause. "Maybe I don't take out a marriage license first, but I sure as hell have to like a woman a lot beforehand. And I like you a lot. You like me just as much. Simmer down."

Rianna grabbed up her coffee cup and fled. "I'll be in the shower if my father calls."

"He won't get through if he does."

Rianna paused in midflight and turned. "Why not?"

"I unplugged the phones." Ty's tone softened. "A little bonus, compliments of your bodyguard. You needed nonstop sleep and I made sure you got it, Rainbow."

RIANNA TOOK the hottest shower her skin could stand and asked herself if Ty knew how she melted each time he called her Rainbow. Had he any idea how connected it made her feel to him, to his childhood and his optimistic grandmother?

By the time she'd dressed in jeans and sweater, she had concluded that each time that nickname passed his lips, some part of Ty melted, too.

Rianna resolved yet again that for all the melting going on between Ty and herself, none of it would lead to the logical conclusion. So they liked each other enough to want to make love. In two days it had come to that. She could admit it as well as Ty. However, wanting and doing were two different things—she planned to keep that fact firmly in mind.

"We have to buy groceries sometime today," Ty announced when she returned to the kitchen and found him making French toast. "This is the last of the eggs and bread. We'll need milk, too, before long."

"Have you plugged the phones back in?" Rianna asked, noting that he had already set the table.

"No. I figured two arguments before breakfast would be one too many for your overwrought nerves."

"I'm sorry I flipped out earlier, Ty."

Ty handed her a plate of toast and turned back to fill his own. "You had reason. I didn't really want to sleep alone. You slept better with me than you do alone, didn't you?"

There was no denying it, so she sat down at the table and admitted, "If I didn't have a call from Father to worry about, I'd feel wonderful right now about sleeping all night."

"You'd feel perfect if something had happened," he asserted, his back to her. "So would I."

Rianna couldn't refute that. Nor could she help lifting her eyes from the toast she was dousing with syrup to look at Ty. She saw muscles ripple and flex across his broad, bare back as he rinsed the frying pan under the tap, then dried his hands. From every angle he was heaven.

He scooped up his plate and joined her at the table. "Does that look mean you agree?" he inquired with a teasing smile. "Don't blush and look down. When was the last time you had a man in your bed, Rianna?"

"I thought we were finished with this subject, Ty. Don't you ever stick to any agreement you make?"

"I never agreed not to talk about it."

"Eat your breakfast instead. It's delicious. You're an excellent cook."

"I'm an even better lover. So are you."

Rianna slammed her fork onto her plate. "Why are you doing this? Baiting me like this?"

"Because you flounced out before I could tell you I want you more than any woman I've ever known and it's driving me crazy. I want you so much that I didn't do anything I was burning to do in your bed. Give me a little credit."

Rianna took a deep, bracing breath. "Listen to me, Ty. I haven't had a man in my bed since Brent. I haven't wanted any man I've met since then—until you." She pushed her chair back and stood. "Yes, I want you as much as you want me. But more than that I want to tell my father when he calls that you and I are friends—just that. I've never lied to him and I don't want to start now."

Ty sighed. "Sit down and finish up before you rush off to plug in the phone. Your toast is getting cold."

"Only if you drop the subject."

"I'll drop it," he said. "But it won't go away!"

With the meal over and the dishes washed, Ty plugged in the phone. It remained silent for a good hour afterward, during which Rianna resumed work on Squeeze's portrait and Ty showered and shaved.

He had just settled down at the table in the studio with a box of slides and a viewer, when the phone at his elbow rang.

"Shall I tell him you're out?" Ty poised a hand over the receiver.

Rianna shook her head and slid off her stool. "He'll turn purple if he knows you're here."

Four more rings sounded before she could force herself to answer. "Hello?"

Ty stood and pressed her down onto his stool. He kept his hands on her shoulders.

"Hi! Hold on a sec." She covered the mouthpiece and smiled at Ty. "It's Chloe, Gordo's fiancée."

"Want me to leave?"

"No. I won't be long." She lifted her hand from the receiver. "How was your trip? Did you find a dress?"

Ty lingered behind Rianna, then reached out and gently began massaging her shoulders and the base of her neck as she talked and listened. From her responses to Chloe he got the gist of the call. The trip to San Francisco had been quite eventful, since she'd only found the wedding dress she wanted after an exhausting search.

"Chloe, it sounds scrumptious," Rianna told her friend, letting her head loll back as Ty's moving thumbs and fingers worked their magic. "Can't wait to see it." She was silent for a moment. "Right now? You have it there at the gallery with you? Well, I guess I... well, sure. We—I have to get groceries, anyway. Sure. Fifteen minutes or so, I guess. Okay, see ya soon. Bye."

She hung up and leaned forward to let Ty work on her upper spine.

"Feel good?"

"Wonderful. How did you learn to do this?"

"By osmosis. I get a massage three times a week at my athletic club when I'm in the city. Takes the kinks out after pumping iron."

"You lift weights?" It was hard to imagine; he was making her feel weightless as well as boneless.

"I work out three times a week. I'm off schedule now and I can already feel it." He laughed. "I'll have love handles before the week is out."

"You won't if you use the Soloflex muscle machine that's collecting dust in my storeroom while you're here." It was getting harder by the minute to form words. Oh, his fingers knew every spot where tension could lurk and massaged it out.

"A Soloflex, huh? Why don't you use it?"

"After I bought it, I found out that I'd rather run."

"You wouldn't mind if I set it up?"

"Not at all. There's plenty of room in here."

"I'll do that then, when we get back."

"From where?" she murmured, her eyes closed, her entire back given up to Ty to manipulate as he wished.

"From Chloe's, where we're supposed to be in about twelve minutes, from what I could gather."

"Oh . . . that's right. . . ." She felt Ty kneel behind her and curl his hands around her upper arms, felt him draw her back against his chest.

"You smell so good, Rainbow," he whispered into her ear. "You feel so good wherever I touch you."

He had rendered her so limp and relaxed that she leaned back against him now without protest and let him whisper into the curve of her throat that he thought her the sexiest woman in the world. She was so relaxed that she let his lips travel that soft curve down and back up, where he nipped at her ear and touched his tongue to the tiny hole in her earlobe.

"You need moments like this in your life, Rianna. We both do." He pressed a hard kiss against the side of her throat, slid his hands under her arms and rested them just under her breasts. From massaging her back he knew that she wore no bra under her sweater.

"Ty...what are you doing?" She placed her hands upon his, felt the heat of his body surround her just as his arms did.

"You know what I'm doing." He kept kissing her neck, tracing the shape of her ear with the tip of his tongue.

"Yes, but..." She felt too weak to break his embrace, strong enough only to slide her fingers into the spaces between his and urge up his hands, up to where her quivering flesh craved his touch.

His palms curved beneath her breasts and cupped them. "No, don't," he whispered when she lifted her hands from his. "Leave your fingers on mine. Feel your beauty through me. You are so beautiful, my Rainbow."

Her fingers moved in tandem with his as he found her nipples and circled them through her sweater. She felt the hammer of his heart against her back. Or was it her own heart that was racking her ribs from front to back? She didn't know. There was no knowing anything but the arousing friction of Ty's flattened palms on her breasts, the swirl of his tongue in her ear.

"Ty, Chloe expects me...." Even as she murmured the reminder, she arched her back, offering herself wholly to the pleasure he was giving her.

"We'll go in a minute." Even as he promised it, he slid his hands free and lifted the hem of her sweater. "In a minute..."

Then he was touching her bare skin, stroking each breast, rolling the budded tips between thumb and forefinger until Rianna's hands joined his and pressed them to her to halt the sensual onslaught.

"Ty, stop."

"Tell me you don't love it and I will."

"I can't. I do. But stop now, please."

"Just for now or for always?"

"For now...I don't know."

Ty slowly withdrew his hands and turned her to face him. "Let me know when you know," he murmured, standing and pulling her to her feet with him.

She swayed, his arms looped around and held her close. He dropped one hand from her waist, slid it into the back pocket of her jeans and pressed her lower body to his own.

"You just let me know," he repeated softly. "I'll be as ready as I am now."

Rianna buried her face against his shirt. The hard jut of his erection made her acknowledge that it would be up to her to choose.

It was impossible to believe she'd only known Ty two days. Easy to believe that if Chloe hadn't been waiting, she'd have gone straight over the edge with him, right there in her studio. The bedroom would have been too far away.

The phone rang and she pulled out of Ty's arms to turn and stare at it.

Behind her Ty said, "Whether that's my office or your father, we're not home right now. Are we?"

"No," she agreed, moving away from the phone. "We're out seeing Chloe and grocery shopping and messing up your room at La Playa."

Her phone was still ringing when they set out on the ten-minute walk downtown to the art gallery that Chloe Osborne managed. Five minutes gone, they ran into Mame coming out of a posh beauty salon.

"We simply have to stop colliding like this," Mame drawled. She looked slyly from Ty to Rianna. "And where are you trotting off to today?"

"To see Chloe," Rianna told her aunt.

"At the gallery?"

"Yes."

Ty linked his arm with Rianna's and said, "We're late getting there. You don't mind if we trot on, do you?"

"Not at all. Trot on. Ta."

Ty glanced over his shoulder as he led Rianna away. "She's going back into the shop," he muttered.

Rianna shrugged. "Maybe she forgot something."

"Yeah. Like making a quick phone call to let someone know you didn't dump me last night."

"It won't make things any worse if she is." Rianna sighed.

They walked on for a block, then Ty pulled her to a stop. "Things are worse than you know, Rainbow."

"What do you mean? How can they be?"

"Easy. Your father and I have tangled before. When you were in Kenya."

"What are you talking about?"

"Let's sit down for a minute." He led her to an empty sidewalk bench and continued. "I knew when you didn't recognize my name right off that you hadn't played catch-up with the six months of local news you missed while you were gone. If you had, you'd have remembered Tyler Toranaga."

Rianna remembered him saying he'd been written about before. She frowned. "What happened?"

"Police brutality charge." He drew in a deep breath. "I shot a twelve-year-old kid in the line of duty. I was undercover. It was dark, after midnight on a heroin bust with Biff Gallagher and a backup squad car. Just as we rushed the target house, what looked like a man came out, pointing a pistol. He was five-ten, solid build, and just kept coming after two halt commands. Biff's gun jammed. Mine didn't."

"Oh, Ty." She took his hand into hers and sat in silence with him for a few moments. "You know, I thought your name sounded familiar at first, but I couldn't connect it to anything but *Shogun.* I *do* vaguely recall reading something else with that name in it now." She thought hard. "It was after I got back from Africa. A short follow-up article or something in a newspaper."

"Not Nathan Breece's papers. There weren't any follow-ups in them about me being cleared after a six-month investigation. There were only headlines and editorials when it happened. You can imagine how your father's editorials attacked the brutal Japanese cop who shot a defenseless kid pointing a toy pistol at him in the dark. No mention in Nathan Breece's editorials that I shot to wound, not to kill. No mention that the kid was out of the hospital in two days and back playing tough with a real pistol a week later."

"Ty, that's terrible. I'm sorry."

"Me, too. The smaller newspapers got the story straight. Sure, I had a reputation for being something of a maverick when it came to following the letter of the law. But to read your dad's editorials, I was a loose cannon. He wanted to ride me out of the police force on a rail and he almost did it. You can't tell me a white cop would've gotten the headlines I did."

"You're probably right," Rianna said. "But that's past history."

"Not for me it isn't. You can bet it isn't for Nathan Breece, either. He doesn't like to lose."

"I know, Ty. I know. He's never given up his battle with me, either."

"What battle?"

"The one to convince me that I'd be happier following in his footsteps with the papers than I am painting animals. You don't know how many times I've wished

I had a sister or brother who lived and breathed news-print. Father's the heir to a communications dynasty and craves an heir of his own. All he got was an artist."

"And a damned fine one, too," Ty rejoined. "Doesn't that count for anything with him?"

"Oh, he's proud of my accomplishment. He just doesn't think it holds a candle to running a news em-pire."

Ty shook his head and squeezed her hand. "You know, the day I first staked you out, I thought you thought like a Breece. I thought you were a trust-fund brat who dabbled in art for something to do and merely happened to be good at it. I wasn't prepared to like or respect you one bit."

"Should I be sorry I disappointed you?" Rianna in-quired with a small smile.

"Maybe. You're not quite what my parents would expect I'd bring home for dinner."

"You're not the only one who's disappointed in the wrong way. I can't invite you home to dinner with Fa-ther, either. It would break his heart."

"Good thing we're not in love and don't want to get married, isn't it?" Ty said lightly, though there was nothing at all buoyant in the way he felt.

"Isn't it, though?" affirmed Rianna, matching his tone. "We'll have to keep it that way."

"Friends, you mean. Like we were last night and this morning."

"Look, Ty. I know there's no going back from here. That doesn't mean we can't keep the brakes on from now on, does it?"

"All I can say is mine keep slipping, no matter how hard I step on them. Yours aren't holding any better."

"I've only known you two days."

"We've covered a lot of ground in that time."

"We're all wrong for each other."

"Yep. Wrong name, wrong race. Opposite sides of the dollar sign. Substantial reasons to not get involved. And you know what else?"

"What?"

Ty stood up and held out his hand. "Chloe's going to think we got run over."

They walked on. Rianna turned over in her mind all the wrongs that couldn't keep her from feeling so right with Ty. She watched her feet on the sidewalk, matching steps with his. So right. Yes, here she was in one of the most romantic places in the world, walking along a quaint street crammed with tiny shops and hideaway restaurants, on the arm of a man who loved rainbows and animals and dancing the night away. Very, very right.

Chloe's art gallery was tucked away at the end of a charming cobblestoned alley. Mornings were always slow for her business and today was no exception. She was straightening a Miró print on a wall hung with abstracts when Rianna and Ty walked in.

"About time," she said, smoothing her brown Dutch-boy bob. "I was ready to send the cops on a search and rescue. What held you up?"

"Mame," Rianna fibbed. "We bumped into her on the way and you know Mame."

Chloe rolled her huge brown eyes. "Sometimes I wish I didn't. She's going to hate my dress. 'Not a designer original, darling.'"

They all laughed and Rianna introduced Ty, whose hand Chloe shook as she gave him a friendly, open smile. That was Chloe, Rianna thought with warm affection for her future cousin-in-law who, at five foot one, was one of the few adults she could top in height.

Heightwise there were few odder-looking couples than Chloe and Gordo, yet Rianna had always considered them a perfect match. She could see now from Chloe's expression that she approved of Ty.

When Chloe unveiled her lovely antique-lace wedding dress in the back room for Ty and Rianna to admire, there was a moment when Rianna's throat tightened at the memory of her own bridal gown—now ashes, for she had burned it. She lifted her chin and saw Ty looking at her with compassion. He smiled slightly, a smile she knew was meant to buck her up.

"Did Rianna tell you she's a bridesmaid?" Chloe asked Ty.

"No, she didn't get around to telling me that yet."

"Ty's vacationing here," Rianna put in quickly. "We just met a few days ago."

"On the beach walk," Ty added. He touched the bandage on his forehead. "I had a fall and she came to my rescue."

"Ah," said Chloe, looking from Ty to Rianna as if she, too, could sense their attraction to each other. "I see."

The phone on the wall rang. Chloe answered it and held out the receiver to Ty.

"It's for you. A man."

He took it. "Ty Toranaga here."

"Keep pushing and you'll get shoved," a male voice growled. Ty heard a click as the phone was hung up.

"Okay," he replied. "Sure. I suspected he would. I'll give him a call." Careful to keep his expression impassive, he replaced the receiver. "My office," he told Chloe. "I left word I'd be here after Rianna invited me along. Hope you don't mind."

"Not at all," said Chloe, turning back to sigh again over the lacy wonder of her wedding dress.

Rianna directed a quizzical look at Ty. "But how did your—?"

An abrupt shake of his head stopped her. He touched a finger to his lips and shot her a look over Chloe's bent head. *Later,* his expression said. She closed her mouth and glanced at Chloe, who was still dreamily examining her gown.

Later, Rianna agreed in silence with a slight nod at Ty. *Later.*

7

"HOW DID your office call you at the gallery?" Rianna asked the minute she and Ty had left Chloe's and were on their way again. "You didn't leave word."

"That wasn't my office."

"Not your . . . ? Who, then?"

"I don't know." Ty repeated the caller's message and described the voice.

"Oh, brother!" Rianna exclaimed. "Welcome to life with Father. Mame called him from the beauty shop and tattled. You were right about why she went back in."

"You think that was your father threatening me?"

"It had to be. Who else knew we were at the gallery but Mame?"

Ty looked around. "You never know."

Rianna saw only a Carmel sidewalk peopled with the typical mix of tourists and locals. She shrugged and reminded herself that Ty was always checking things out.

"It was Father," she assured him. "When I left home after college, he was terrified I'd be kidnapped, like Patty Hearst once was. I refused to hire protection, but that didn't stop him. He hired two men to monitor me from a distance twenty-four hours a day. They parked in front of my apartment, followed me everywhere for months. They never made a secret of it and I couldn't do a thing to stop them. For all I know my phone was tapped, too. I had to threaten to leave the country before he finally called them off."

"I can't fault his concern for you, Rianna. A lot of ordinary people maintain better personal security than you do. With no burglar alarm in your house and a listed phone number you're taking chances that any single woman, not to mention one named Breece, shouldn't take. The way you live you're an easy target."

"I live the way the majority of ordinary people do," Rianna objected. "I already told you, most of my life I was locked in, watched over and chauffeured wherever I went. Well, no one's going to cramp my style again, if I can help it. I'll take my chances along with the rest."

Ty scowled. "Thanks for reminding me how very welcome I am at the moment."

"I didn't mean you, Ty. You're . . . different."

Ty shoved his hands into his pockets and hunched forward. "What I heard was that different or not, you'd rather I was out of the picture. You'd rather gamble that it was an ex-con who murdered Al. You'd rather gamble with your life that you're not next."

Rianna hooked one hand around his elbow and pulled him around to face her. "You wouldn't be here with me right now if I wanted to take that chance, though I'm beginning to wonder at the concerns you've expressed. You haven't come up with much evidence that I have a lot to worry about."

"Want to see some real soon?" Ty inquired, his voice low. "Don't look now, but we've been tailed since we came out of the alley."

"Tailed? By whom?"

Ty pulled her close and commanded in a harsh whisper, "No, don't look yet. You'll give us away."

"Who is it?"

"Keep calm. Do what I say. Now, I'm going to kiss you in a second and make it look real. When I let you go, look around as if you're embarrassed. He's wearing a Giants baseball cap and a gray windbreaker."

There in the middle of the sidewalk Ty lowered his mouth to hers. Rianna closed her eyes, torn between welcoming the intimate contact and hoping passersby wouldn't stop and stare at the public spectacle they were making of themselves.

She was already blushing from the heat of her response to Ty's kiss when he lifted his head with unconcealed reluctance and whispered against her lips, "Now look around."

It took a moment for her to focus. Yes, there was the man. He had the beefy look of a heavyweight boxer.

Draping his arm over Rianna's shoulders and moving on down the sidewalk, Ty asked, "Get a good look at our Giants fan?"

"He looks like a tourist."

"You're dead wrong."

"How do you know?"

"Because he stopped to browse a shop window when we stopped to browse one. We crossed the street, he crossed the street, always the same distance behind. There's no mystery if you have an eye for it."

"How did you catch on so quickly?"

"Experience." Ty tightened his arm around her. "I'm not going to let anything happen to you. Don't you worry."

"I'm more furious than worried. I had hoped Father was through butting into my personal life, but apparently he's not. He's obviously hired this man to keep him informed of whatever I do with my new friend."

"You think he'd go that far?"

"If he thinks *I'm* going too far, absolutely."

"Maybe you're right."

"It makes perfect sense," Rianna said firmly. "Mame saw us together last night and by morning we're being followed and getting threatening phone calls. That was our new constant companion who called you—from the public phone in the coffee shop next to the gallery, I'll bet."

"It's possible," Ty mused. "It's also possible that what I suspected might occur is happening."

"No, Ty. Father's done this before and he's doing it again."

"There's got to be a way we can find out for sure," Ty said after a pause for thought. "But how?"

"I'll simply accuse him of it when he calls and see what he says," Rianna declared.

"What if he denies it? Would he lie?"

She considered that at length. "Ordinarily I don't think so. There's nothing ordinary about me being with you, though. He might deny it in this case, even if it's true."

"Back to square one again," Ty observed.

"Let's think over a cup of coffee at the pub," she suggested. "My friend Cybil tends bar there."

He gave her a dry look. "That's something I already know, remember?"

"Sometimes I'd rather forget how much you know about me."

"You'd be better off hoping the guy behind us doesn't know the half of it."

She cast another glance over her shoulder, then hopefully studied Ty. "Maybe you're mistaken just this once. Maybe he isn't following us at all."

He wore a reproachful air as they entered the wood-paneled pub. "Watch him suddenly acquire a raging thirst for a draft beer. Just watch."

Ty was right. They had barely exchanged greetings with Cybil and occupied a leather-upholstered booth by a corner window when their beefy watchdog strolled in. He took a stool at the end of the bar, ordered a beer, and evidenced a keen interest in the tennis match playing on the wide-screen TV.

"At least he's out of earshot," Ty muttered. "Unless he can read lips, which he doesn't look sharp enough to do. He's not wearing a piece, fortunately."

"A piece?"

"A gun."

"Oh." For the first time Rianna felt strangely comforted that Ty's gun was snug in the holster hidden under his leather jacket.

"Say there," drawled tall, redheaded Cybil after she had brought them coffee and been introduced to Ty. "Weren't you at Nepenthe last week without that bandage on your forehead?"

Ty nodded and Cybil inclined her head in a knowing gesture. "Thought so," she said. "So were we." She winked an emerald eye at Rianna. "Weren't we?"

"Really?" Ty said, looking the total innocent.

"Really." Cybil grinned at Rianna. "Was I right or was I right?"

"Maybe, maybe not." Rianna shrugged and tried to look blasé, which succeeded only in widening her friend's grin and inviting another question.

"How did all of this come about, you two? Forget free refills if you don't tell."

Ty pointed to the bandage on his forehead. "I fell hard for her on the beach walk. She noticed."

"Do tell. Well, well. How romantic. Just let me know when you need a free refill, folks."

"We'll do that, Cybil," Rianna promised, her tone wry as she watched her savvy friend saunter back to tend bar.

"What's she so smug about?" Ty asked.

"Nothing."

"I've never seen 'nothing' make you blush like that." He was silent for a moment, studying Rianna's face.

"You blushed the same way that day she pointed me out to you at Nepenthe, you know."

"I didn't."

Ty reached out and took her hand. "You did. You looked flustered as hell. Why?"

Rianna sighed; Ty didn't give up easily. After their embrace in the studio, she knew how his touch could coax and persuade. He was wearing her down already, stroking her fingers, her palm, her inner wrist.

"You're turning pink. Why, Rainbow?"

What was the use? "Because she picked you out of the lunch crowd there as the perfect man for me, if you can imagine."

He didn't say anything for a minute. "She may have been on to something. When I kissed you out there, I felt like the perfect man with the perfect woman."

With effort, Rianna detached her hand from his and wrapped it around her coffee cup. "Don't make things more impossible than they are, Ty. We didn't come here to discuss how we feel about each other."

"Right." He drummed his fingers on the table where hers had been, then pulled back his hand from that spot. "We came to decide how to smoke out who's paying our friend to dog our heels. Any ideas?"

"Nothing brilliant at the moment. How about you?"

He shook his head. "I shouldn't have kissed you out there. I've only been able to think half-straight ever since."

"Me, too," Rianna admitted glumly. "No more love scenes on the sidewalk for either of us, all right?"

"All ri—" Ty shopped short and looked up. "Wait a minute." He snapped his fingers. "Why not? That's it."

"What's it?"

Ty leaned forward. "Listen, what would he do if he thought you were off the deep end over me? Not just dating me, but heavy, serious stuff?"

"Who?"

"Your father."

"Well, he's already ringing my phone off the hook and having me followed. He'll demand that I stop seeing you, as it is."

"What if you don't?"

Without a moment's hesitation Rianna replied, "He'll fly down in his private jet and pay me a personal visit to make sure I get the message."

Ty nodded as if he fully expected her reply. "That's what we have to do, then."

"For heaven's sake, *what* do we have to do?"

He reached into his pocket and threw a bill and some change onto the table. "On the off chance that our leech reads lips, let's talk outside."

Rianna managed only a quick farewell wave in Cybil's general direction before she found herself walking smartly down the sidewalk with Ty's arm around her.

"What we're going to do," Ty said, "is give our friend behind us every reason to think we're madly in love. How long would it take Nathan to jet down if he knew we were all over each other in public?"

"He'd be here by the weekend at the latest."

"Good. If he comes down to personally twist your arm—or mine—we can relax about our goon back there. If he doesn't . . ."

Rianna's steps slowed as the implications of what he was proposing sank in. "Ty, that's living too dangerously for me."

He rejected her objection with a squeeze of her shoulders that drew her flush against his side. "Not as dangerous as it already is if our new friend had a hand in Al's death. I can't go off half-cocked, jumping to conclusions. I have to know exactly who I'm dealing with," he insisted. "Infuriating your father is a surefire way to find out fast."

"It can't be the only way," she protested, unable to keep what she knew was a note of both desperation and anticipation from filtering into her voice.

"Name another."

"Well, we could . . ." She racked her brain and drew a series of blanks. Could what? She couldn't name anything that would enrage her father more than knowing his only daughter was in love with an ex-cop named Tyler Toranaga.

"Let's give it a shot," Ty prodded, "starting right now."

"How?"

"Like this." He drew her toward a little rock cave that formed the recessed entrance to an haute cuisine French restaurant that was closed at that hour.

Rianna dragged her feet. "What are we doing?"

Ty pulled her with him into the shaded grotto. "Listen, from now on we're doing everything lovers do in romantic Carmel. We're going to linger over candlelight dinners holding hands. We're going to make out on the beach. We're going to duck into hidden doorways like this to steal a quick kiss. Or a long one."

He leaned out far enough to look down the sidewalk, then drew back and murmured, "He's hot on our trail. Kiss me."

"What?"

"Shh. Put your arms around my neck."

When she hesitated to obey his command, he did it for her, lifting her hands to his shoulders and pressing her back against the rough stone wall. His chest had begun to flatten her breasts, his lips had started their first descent to hers when she heard heavy footsteps approach on the sidewalk, then slow to a stop just short of the grotto. She heard the strike of a match and realized the man was probably leaning against the building, smoking a cigarette.

"Mmm, sweet. I could kiss you all day," Ty said, just loud enough for an intent eavesdropper to hear. He slid his hands down the length of her sweatered arms and curved his palms to the shape of her rib cage, where his thumbs framed the soft side swells of her unconfined breasts. "Are you with me, Rainbow?" he whispered—for her ears alone.

"Do I have a choice?" she inquired in return.

"It's yours. Yes or no?"

"Here goes," she murmured and lifted her lips into his kiss. At first it was the barest of warm contacts. Heaven. Rianna cradled one hand around the back of Ty's head and drew him down to taste her again and again until there was no breaking apart.

All that should have been on her mind faded away—leaving only the sandalwood scent of Ty's after-shave and the sensations aroused by the muscular body pressed to hers, the restless thumbs upon her breasts as erotic and exciting as the tongue swirling around in her mouth.

They separated by mutual consent, shaking and shaken. Ty's expression, Rianna knew, mirrored the sheer amazement she felt. They had forgotten everything but each other, though people passed by on the sidewalk—even the man loitering and listening out of sight.

Ty rested his forehead against Rianna's. She knew what he was thinking. Their kiss had begun as the first act in a charade, one calculated to mislead. The man following them couldn't doubt what had transpired. But it had been no act. Not in the least.

"Where were we headed before we got sidetracked?" Ty murmured.

"To your hotel, I think."

"Ah, yes." He quirked an eyebrow in the direction of their unseen eavesdropper to indicate for whom his next words were intended. "My room, a place whose time has come, I believe?"

"Most definitely," Rianna agreed, reluctantly slipping her hands from the back of Ty's neck to the front of his leather jacket. It had felt so right to furrow his thick black hair with her fingers, to crush herself against his strength and hold on for dear life.

Yet what he felt for her or she for him wasn't love, she reminded herself when Ty led her out of the shady cavern into the cool April sunshine. It couldn't be love this fast, this soon. Naturally they would pretend it was—for the benefit of their constant companion. But it wasn't love. No. Though far more than lust, it was not the real thing.

Still, it was powerful enough to convince her that she couldn't continue charades with Ty on this scale for very long. He kissed her twice more on the walk to the hotel—a short, sweet pluck of the lips on a street corner being followed by an embrace in an out-of-the-way phone booth.

Desperate for an alternative ploy by the time they reached his room, she insisted, "There must be some safer way to flush Father out."

Ty looked up from vigorously unmaking his bed for the benefit of the maid. "Define 'safer.'"

"Safer than what we both know is foreplay, whatever good reason we have to be doing it."

"You can't say it's not enjoyable as well as reasonable."

"Dangerous is the word for it, Ty."

"Throw in arousing and crazy-making while you're at it. We're a championship pair when it comes to kissing."

"That's why there has to be another way," she replied, trying to put a warning into her tone.

"If Nathan's the hothead you say he is, we won't be foreplaying much longer." Ty went back to scrunching and bunching the sheets and bedspread.

"I think I should confront him on this before we do any more kissing," she persisted.

"And if he doesn't admit he put this hound on our trail, what then?"

"Ty, I can't take it."

He threw a pillow at her. "You don't like the way I kiss?"

She threw it back at him. "It should be outlawed, as you well know."

"You could look a little happier about it." He squeezed the smooth pillow in his hands like an accordion.

"And *you* could stop grinning as if you're enjoying every minute of it."

"I am. I love the way you kiss. I love knowing we can do it again and again, all the way home."

"What happens when we get home, Ty? Who's going to turn off the heat?"

Ty pointed at the phone. "Call your father right now, if you're that uptight about it. Confront him. Accuse him. Get it over with."

"When we get home I will. I like to be in my own comfort zone when I butt heads with my father."

"Having butted heads with him in print, I can't say I blame you. But the charade continues between here and home. If he confesses on the phone, we'll call it off. If not, I don't know what else to do but keep it up until something—or nothing—happens."

He went in to steam up the bathroom and dampen towels, leaving Rianna to contemplate the ravaged bed and imagine herself lying there naked in his strong arms. She heard the spray of the shower and pictured taking one with him. To distract herself, she walked over to the window where she stared out at the vast expanse of the Pacific Ocean and remembered the double rainbow off the coast at Nepenthe the first day she'd seen Ty.

It seemed now that it had been a portent of significance, signaling Ty's entry into her life. Did he remember those two arcs and attribute any special significance to their appearance, too?

Probably he did, for he wasn't just any man. He was Ty, who had believed as a boy that wishes on rainbows were wishes come true. Ty, who had mingled his tears of grief with hers. Ty, whose presence in her life after only three days was making her wish that wishes *did* come true. For others, she reflected, perhaps they did. Wishing was futile for Ty and herself.

Then his voice at her ear rumbled, "Remember that double rainbow at Nepenthe?"

"Don't *do* that!" she exclaimed, lurching around and clutching her throat. "Make a sound or something before you ambush."

He cupped a hand to her cheek in a gesture of apology. "I didn't realize you were that lost in thought."

She turned away from the sensory allure of his touch to take in the view again, then asked, "How did you know I was thinking about that day at Nepenthe?"

"Maybe because I'm reminded of it when I look out this window myself." He stood behind her and closed his hands around her upper arms. "I'll never see a rainbow again that won't make me think of you, Rianna Breece."

"And I'll never forget that wishes on rainbows are wishes come true, Tyler Toranaga. Even if your grandmother *was* wrong." She let herself sway back for a moment.

"It's hard to believe we'll someday only be memories to each other," Ty said, slipping his hands down to span her waist and hold her against him.

"There's no use in believing we'll be anything more, Ty."

"We could let ourselves believe for the time being." Keeping his hands on her waist, he moved in front of her, blocking the view with his broad shoulders.

Rianna closed her eyes to escape the desire she saw in his and whispered, "We both know we're all wrong for each other."

"Emotionally and physically we're more than right," Ty pressed. "We like being together, doing things together. Something hits us both broadside every time we kiss. We could let ourselves believe..."

"It's physical attraction," she countered. "Sexual chemistry."

Ty was silent for a long pause. "It's more than that for both of us. If we weren't who we are, we'd be proving it's more in that bed over there."

She stepped out of his grasp. "Let's go home first and find out what Father has to say for himself."

"Rianna—"

"We are who we are, Ty. Let's go."

"Not yet."

"Why not?"

"It's too soon."

"For what? The bed's a mess. The bathroom is, too. We're finished here."

"Rianna, we've been here all of twenty minutes."

"So?"

"So imagine how it's going to look to our friend downstairs if we leave this soon after arriving." Ty's lips curved into a slow grin. "He'll tell your father that his daughter's new lover is trigger-happy. We wouldn't want Nathan thinking that. He'll decide he has nothing to worry about."

"He'll be worried enough when he hears I was here with you for a quickie. He doesn't have to think you're a marathon man on top of it all."

"I don't want him thinking I'm a minuteman, either. Believe me, Rainbow, trigger-happy isn't my style."

"Tell you what," she said, "I'll look so blitzed on the way out that he'll think *I'm* the one with the short fuse."

"We should stay here at least an hour."

"And do what, besides the obvious? Watch soap operas and game shows on TV?"

"We could have lunch sent up."

"I'm not hungry."

"What you are is afraid—afraid that what's right between us will take over."

"Aren't *you*, Ty?"

"I have my fears," he admitted, "but they aren't curbing what I feel. All I think about is making love with you. I'm thinking about it right now."

"*I* think we'd better go."

Ty reluctantly agreed and they left his hotel room.

They made their way out after collecting Ty's messages at the desk. Their shadow was in an armchair, reading a newspaper. A few feet beyond where he sat, Rianna drew Ty to a halt and gave him a long, soulful kiss.

"Three times!" she exclaimed, loud enough for listening ears to hear. "How *does* my samurai do it?"

"Must be in my genes," Ty returned, blinking in astonishment at her audacity.

Rianna emitted a velvety female growl of appreciation and slowly let her eyes trace a path down the front of Ty's leather jacket to the black denims he wore.

"It's in your jeans, all right," she said, almost purring. "It most certainly is, Toranaga *San*."

Ty suppressed his mirth until he and Rianna were out of the hotel and walking away, then began to shake. "In my jeans! I can't believe you said that."

"Father won't either when he hears it secondhand."

"He'll only have a contract out on my life by morning, that's all," Ty groaned.

Rianna laughed, feeling naughty as well as witty. She squeezed her arm around his waist, her eyes merry. "You wanted to look good, didn't you?"

"Not *that* good." He threw back his head and laughed even harder.

"It's your own fault for handing me the perfect straight line, Toranaga *San*."

"You started before that," he countered. "*Three!* I was so stunned, I said the first thing that entered my head."

"You can't blame me for making good use of it," she crowed.

"Did you see his eyes almost pop out of his head?" Ty wiped a gleeful tear from his own eyes.

Rianna dissolved into a fit of giggles against him. "He's definitely wondering what you did to me in that twenty minutes. Is he still a respectful distance behind us?"

"Very respectful. And wondering all the way."

"I can just see his report to San Francisco," she said, chortling as she remembered the man's boggled expression. "Will he phone it in or fax it, do you think?"

"Fax." Ty whooped. "That way he can title it The Twenty-Minute Workout."

Rianna felt as if her sides were beginning to split. "It'll scorch the paper in the fax machine."

"And set off the smoke detector."

"I can see it now."

"Me, too."

"He'll put it all in one sentence!" she gasped. "It'll say, 'Multiple kisses on the way to the hotel room and multiple org—org—'"

"'Orgasms in it,'" Ty hooted.

They staggered to their destination, a corner grocery store, convulsed by bursts of laughter. They had to separate in the store to sober up. Ty took the bakery aisle, while Rianna headed for the dairy cases.

By the time they were reunited in canned goods, they had each regained control of a sort. Somehow they gathered up what they needed, paid for it, and escaped before they ended up rolling in the aisles.

On the sidewalk, each clutching a paper grocery sack, they caught sight of their friend and broke up all over again.

When they reached the cottage, the persistent ringing of the telephone immediately sobered them up.

"Uh-oh. Time to face the music," said Ty, reaching for Rianna's grocery sack. "You go. I'll put this stuff away."

She used the phone in the studio.

"Where in blazes have you been?" her father thundered.

"It's nice to talk to you, too, Father," she replied archly. "How are you?"

"On the verge of a heart attack ever since I talked to Mame this morning. Seems she saw you out last night. With a Jap! Name of Toranaga, I believe."

"My friend, Tyler, you mean?"

"No friend of yours or mine! Drop him."

"My friends, Father, are my own business. You haven't even asked me how I am."

"I know how you are. Mame saw Toranaga plastered to you on the dance floor. She knows trouble when she sees it and believe you me, he spells trouble. Shot a defenseless kid when he was a cop here. Steer clear of him."

"I know about the shooting. Ty told me he was cleared of the charges."

"He weaseled out of them," growled Nathan Breece. "He should have had the book thrown at him."

"For what? For shooting in self-defense? Or for being of Japanese origin?"

"You'd have an Uncle Ned and I'd have an older brother if it weren't for them."

"Father," she remonstrated. "I don't choose your friends for you, ever. So don't tell me who I can see and can't see. Furthermore, I don't appreciate your having me followed by your hired hand."

"When have I ever had you followed?"

"Someone has been on my trail ever since Mame reported my social activities to you."

"As usual, you're imagining things."

Rianna shook her head. He always said that when he knew all too well she was right. "Father, I warn you, if anyone you've hired gets within fifty feet of me, I'll sue him for harassment."

"And I'm warning *you*, keep your distance from Toranaga."

"Is that the only reason you called?" Rianna wearily inquired.

"Yes." His voice softened and he changed the subject. "But now that I think of it, why don't you come visit for the weekend? Just the two of us. We'll play a few rounds of golf at the club. I have some people I'd like you to meet."

"Newspaper people, by any chance?"

"Rianna, as I've told you too many times to count, I'm not going to last forever. When my heart gives out, you should be able to take up the reins." His voice cracked. "You're my only child. You're all I've got."

"I know how you feel," Rianna said gently, "and you know how *I* feel. I'd be a disaster at running the business."

"You could be a whiz if you'd put your mind to it."

"I tried that twice as a summer intern. You remember what a mess I made of things both times and how miserable I was. I'm an artist. It's the only work that makes me happy."

"Come up for a good meal and a visit," he invited gruffly. "Get away from Toranaga and let your wise old man talk some common sense into you."

"Not this weekend," she said. "I'm behind on Squeeze-Play's portrait and Gordo's wedding is coming up fast. Which reminds me, I saw Chloe today."

"So I hear."

"From whom?"

"If your friends are none of my business, my business is none of yours."

Rianna rolled her eyes. "Call your spy off my case. And Mame, too. I'm not a child."

"You're the child I love. Promise your poor old father you won't see Toranaga again."

"You know I won't do that."

"Rianna Whitney Breece, do you want me to have a second heart attack?"

"Don't shout, Father, or I'll hang up."

"Shout! I never shout! I *forbid* you to see him, do you hear me? Do you—?"

Rianna hung up, as she always did when he began issuing ultimatums. And as usual, her hands were shaking and her stomach was coiled in knots. In vain she reminded herself how generous her father was in giving to charities, sponsoring food drives for the hungry and homeless via his papers, in lending his name to a multitude of good causes.

She also reminded herself that he really did love her and want the best for her. He always had. He simply didn't comprehend the meaning of the word no unless he was the one saying it.

"Was it as bad as it sounded?" Ty asked when she came into the kitchen. He was sitting at the table, checking through his phone messages from the hotel.

"It's usually that way. He demanded. I refused. He wheedled. I refused. He ranted and raved. I hung up."

"Did he admit to putting a goon on our tail?"

"No. He didn't categorically deny it, either."

"It's still possible that's not his man," Ty said, considering. "If it isn't, I don't want you out of my sight. Understand? Our friend appears to belong to a beige rental car parked just down the street. He's in it now or was when I last looked. I'll call Biff and have him start a search on the license-plate number. Maybe we can get a lead on who he is."

Rianna sat down opposite Ty, propped her elbows upon the table and rested her chin on her clasped hands. She regarded the pile of phone messages in front of him. "If you need to make some calls, feel free."

"He really gets to you, doesn't he?" Ty said, studying her face, then reaching across the table to brush his knuckles over her cheek. "Chin up, Rainbow. You're not the only one in the world who's disappointed dear old Dad. My father doesn't approve of my line of work, either. He and my grandfather were strawberry farmers. You can bet I wasn't reared up to be a cop or a private detective. You and I are both black sheep in our own way."

Ty knew that his parents still felt disappointed that his marriage had failed. They were hoping he'd remarry and start a family. His sister and her husband had already given them three grandchildren. Childless and unmarried, Ty was a continuing worry for them. He knew what they'd say if he brought Rianna Breece home to meet them. Afterward they'd say what Rianna's father had probably already said. *Stick to your own kind.*

"Are you hungry?" Rianna murmured.

"Maybe. I don't know. I can't think when you look at me like that." He brushed his knuckles from her cheek to her wrist and grazed her forearm. "You have the most beautiful eyes."

"Yours are easy to look at, too."

Ty smiled. "Tell me something."

"What?"

"Why do I feel as if I've known you for years instead of days? Why do we get along so well?"

"I don't know, but I feel it, too. A few seconds ago I had kinks in my stomach. Now, after just looking at you I feel better. Much better."

"Think of how much better you'd feel after a hug and a kiss." He grinned and ran his fingertip along her lower lip.

She caught it between her teeth and held it for a moment before letting go. "I think we'd better opt for lunch instead."

"With a nap afterward?" His teasing grin widened.

"Not safe. Will a sandwich and potato chips hold you until dinner?"

"A hug and kiss would hold me better."

"Make your phone calls, Toranaga *San.* I'll make lunch."

Ty pulled a message out of his pile and waved it at her. "Gallagher's offering a free dinner at his house the night after next. Want to go?"

"Not if one extra will be a problem."

"I can't imagine it. Biff and Jeannie love a crowd. That's why they have six kids." He hesitated. "You don't mind kids, do you?"

"I only mind not having a few of my own," Rianna replied, going to the refrigerator.

"You'll have to catch yourself a husband for that," Ty teased, watching the sway of her hips, then added, "Not that I think you'll have any trouble."

"I've had it so far." She turned slightly to look at him. "Do you want children, Ty?"

"Yep. I surely do."

"You'll have to catch yourself a wife for that," she teased in return. "Not that you'll have any trouble."

"I've had it so far. We're two of a kind in more ways than one, aren't we?"

They fell still for a moment, eyes locked, until Rianna pulled hers away and directed them at the phone. "Are you going to return those calls or not?"

"Yeah," he growled, lifting the receiver and punching in the first number. "But I can think of things I'd rather do besides phone work."

8

THE FIRST CALL Ty returned was Biff Gallagher's. After accepting the dinner invitation for Rianna and himself, he enlisted Biff's help with a license-plate search on the beige sedan. Afterward he made several routine business calls.

Rianna prepared sandwiches and herb tea. It was *cozy* to have a man in her sunny kitchen where she always cooked alone. A man like Ty Toranaga, in particular.

The scene was so comfortably domestic that it wasn't at all difficult to imagine Ty as her husband and herself as his wife. She felt him watching her at intervals and wondered if he was having similar thoughts. He blew her a kiss.

Ty had just hung up from his final call when the phone rang. He looked at Rianna. "Your father again, maybe?"

She frowned. "Maybe. He likes to have the last word if he can get it."

Ty picked it up before she could stop him. "Hello?" He signaled to her that it was all right and nodded. "She's right here." Smiling, he held out the receiver. "Gordo."

Breathing a sigh of relief, she took it. "Gordo-guy. What's up?"

"You tell me, Cousin. Who's the deep voice?"

"A friend."

"The one you were with last night?"

"How do you know about last night?"

"Is he?"

"Yes. You've been talking to your mother, haven't you?"

"No, she's been talking to *me*. Grilling me for information is more like it. I pleaded deaf, dumb and blind, even though it sounds as if you've somehow hooked up with Kurt Westwood's bodyguard. What's the story?"

"It's too long to tell on the phone."

"I've got all afternoon. School's out for a district holiday. I'd be spending the latter half with Chloe, but she's got a megabucks art collector coming in after lunch."

Rianna looked at Ty and made a decision against temptation when he blew her another kiss. "Why don't you drop by this afternoon, Gordo? We'll fill you in."

"'We,' eh? I can't wait. You and a man. Together." Gordo chuckled. "Give me an hour. I'll be there."

Rianna and Ty spent that hour talking as they munched sandwiches and chips. She related what it had been like to grow up as an only child in a Nob Hill mansion, to be packed off to boarding school in Switzerland, to vacation at the summer estate on Carmel's posh Seventeen-Mile Drive.

"I was lonely most of the time," she said. "After Mother died, Father tried to be a good parent, but he was too busy to be good at it. He buried his pain in work—the more work, the less pain. Now that I understand why adults cope that way, I don't blame him."

"How did you deal with your own pain at the time?" Ty asked.

"I painted my heart out. It made me feel close to Mother, to all the times we painted together, so I immersed myself in art. I think Father unconsciously objects to my work because it reminds him of her. She was his only great love aside from the news business. Time for a change of subject, I think. What led you into working to protect endangered species, Ty?"

"An albino python and a hyacinth macaw to start with," he replied. "I confiscated them during a dock-warehouse drug bust and got blown away by how beautiful they were. The dealers were smuggling rare birds and reptiles in along with cocaine from South America. Albinos and hyacinths, like the drugs, are banned from import into this country. The smugglers see to it that they get in, though.

"Whether dealing with animals or people, drug dealers are ruthless. The stakes are huge and they want every filthy penny. When their own skins are on the line, though, they'll ditch a boatload worth millions to come up cleanhanded and live to deal again. Figure that an albino python from the wild will bring upwards of $20,000 on the black market and a hyacinth macaw upwards of $10,000. You can see I'm not talking peanuts.

"Long story short, we found the snake and the bird crammed into cages. They could barely move." Ty grimaced at the memory. "Both the cocaine and the cages were weighted so they'd sink fast if they had to be jettisoned."

"That's inhuman!" Rianna exclaimed with a shudder. "Just as horrible as the elephant and rhino poaching I witnessed in Kenya. They're slaughtered only for their tusks and horns and left for the vultures and hyenas."

Ty nodded. "The animals are innocent and helpless. That's why I volunteer what time I can now."

"Perhaps I should, too, considering how closely I'm becoming connected to exotics through my work. It doesn't make sense to paint them if I don't lend a hand in preserving them, does it?"

"You've done a lot already just by painting them so beautifully. Your work leads people to appreciate these magnificent animals and want to preserve them. That's worth a great deal."

"So is the interest from my trust fund," she mused after a moment. "Only my accountant knows that it helps out several museums and art schools, not to mention the homeless on the streets. Maybe endangered species should get a share of the interest, too."

Ty grinned. "You could start with the organization I volunteer for, if you'd like."

"So that's the underlying purpose of all this, is it?" she teased. "You've just been hitting me up for a juicy contribution all this time. You'll be moving out before the ink is dry on my check, won't you?"

Ty leaned forward and snitched a potato chip from her plate. "I'm not moving anywhere, check or no check, until I'm sure you're safe. Besides, I like my new digs and my roommate. Especially my roommate."

It was a good thing that Gordo's knock sounded on the door at that moment, for there was no mistaking what that roguish gleam in Ty's eyes meant. It was far safer to pour Gordo a mug of herb tea, introduce him to Ty and let Ty do the talking.

As Rianna had known they would, the two men hit it off from the start. Ty explained the whole situation and welcomed Gordo's advice. Gordo pledged his silence and support, then their talk turned to basketball.

Basketball led to a discussion of how they worked to stay in shape and before Rianna could quite figure out how it had come about, Ty and Gordo had carted her Soloflex muscle machine from the storeroom into the studio, dusted it off and readied it for action. Soon they were one-upping each other with bench presses and pull-ups.

Gordo was leaving when Ty's office called. Ty waved goodbye from the phone, and Rianna walked her cousin to the door.

"Uncle Nate must be fit to be tied," Gordo observed. "Has he chewed you out yet?"

"'Fit to be tied' is putting it mildly," Rianna replied.

Gordo raised an eyebrow. "He'd be outraged if he saw the way you look at Ty when you think no one's looking. I never saw you look at Brent quite like that."

"Now, Gordo—" she began.

"I'm not blind," he persisted. "Ty looks at you the same way. Forget Uncle Nate and go for it like you did with your work. It's *your* life, not his."

"Gordo, I've broken his heart by living an independent life and painting for a career. I can't totally crush him by getting serious with Ty."

"Would you get serious with him if the situation was different?"

"I . . . might."

"Would. Should."

"He's my only living parent, Gordo. If I ever walk down the aisle again, I want him to give me away with his blessing. You've got things easy with only Mame and her *boys* to handle."

"Not as easy as I wish. She'll *always* regard Chloe as a nobody because Chloe didn't go to the *right* schools, doesn't travel in the *right* circles. . . . Need I go on?"

"Mame *will* come to your wedding, though" was Rianna's pointed reply. "Chloe doesn't have her ethnic origins working against her."

"If she did, she'd still be right for me. I'd bet a hundred to one Toranaga's right for you."

"Gordo, I've known him for three days. You've known him a little over an hour. What basis is that for placing bets?"

"The best when it's pure gut feeling. Hey, I'm the guy who knew I was going to marry Chloe the minute I saw her. We set the date on our first date, remember?"

Rianna hadn't forgotten. Nor had she forgotten unwittingly phoning Gordo the morning after that first date and getting Chloe, still half-asleep, on the other end of the line. They clearly hadn't wasted a moment. Within days they'd been living together.

"I'm not setting any dates with Ty, now or ever," she said firmly. "When this is over, he goes his way and I go mine."

"I hope he goes the way of your bed before then."

"For all you know he has," she retorted, opening the door for him to leave.

"I know what I know," declared Gordo on his way out. "You have a real man in the house, Cousin. Don't waste him on your sofa bed."

During the next few hours Rianna had cause to recall Gordo's parting remark several times. An inordinate number of those recollections occurred during the ninety minutes it took Ty to work out on the Soloflex.

A real man. She tried to paint more of Squeeze-Play while Ty exercised, but she kept peering over the top of her canvas to watch the bunch and bulge and ripple of movement beneath Ty's sweat-sheened skin. He was in superb condition. The triangle of silky black hair between his dark nipples grew damper and darker as he progressed from one set of exercises to the next.

He rested for a few minutes between each set with a white towel hung around his neck. During those intervals Rianna kept her eyes on her canvas, her brush moving. She sensed that Ty looked her way several times. Each time she felt her cheeks flush.

A real man. If only he didn't look good enough to touch and never stop touching. If only he didn't have an infectious sense of humor along with a streak of sensitivity that struck a companion chord in her. If only his confident masculinity didn't make her feel protected and feminine and desirable.

Rianna was still wishing all these things and more when Ty draped the towel around his neck for the last time and ended his exercise session. He sauntered over to her and eyed Squeeze-Play's sinuous, scaly likeness.

"She's coming along, isn't she?"

"Not as well as I'd like."

"How long is she?"

"Ten feet, three inches."

"Gorgeous reptile."

Rianna agreed. "Yes, she's a prime specimen."

"I like her owner a lot, Rainbow."

"Gordo likes you, too. He told me so when he left." *Don't waste him on your sofa bed.*

"At least liking me runs in half of your family."

Unable to resist, she arched an eyebrow at him over her shoulder. "It must be in the genes."

"Where in the jeans?" Ty inquired, snapping an end of his towel gently against the left half of her denim-clad bottom. "I'm partial to the way yours fit, by the way."

"Weren't you headed for the shower?"

"Yeah. A cold one." He snapped the towel. "Again."

"Stop that. I'm trying to paint, Ty."

"Are you going to try until dinner?"

"Yes. Very, very hard."

"Trying won't be the hardest part," Ty advised with a final snap and a snaky grin. "That'll be in my jeans."

HE WORE HIS JEANS to dinner. Rianna wore hers, too. In casual Carmel there were few restaurants that required dressy attire of their patrons. Her suggestion that night was Moroccan, the seating on floor cushions, the eating utensils their hands. The room was small and tent-like, the atmosphere festive with both male and female belly dancers.

After a ritual washing of their hands over a sculpted metal ewer, they were served a bowl of honeyed lamb with almonds, a platter of lemon hare, a chicken pie fragrant with cinnamon and sweetened with powdered sugar.

Gazing around the dimly lit room, Rianna noted aloud that her father's hireling wasn't among the other diners.

"He's loitering around outside, keeping expenses down," Ty said. "Though why he'd cut corners with a billionaire paying his fee is beyond me."

Rianna had only to recall the strict, modest allowance her father had doled out to her during her childhood to know why Nathan Breece might balk at paying expensive restaurant tabs for his paid spies. He had a solid respect for money.

"And here we thought we'd have to smooch our way through dinner for his benefit," she commented with a sidelong flash of the eyes at Ty.

Ty met it with a level glance that held her eyes across the round brass tray on short legs that served as their table. "Is that relief I hear? Or regret?"

She couldn't look away. "A little of each."

"More regret than relief, if I'm hearing right," he said.

"Maybe."

"Maybe, hell. Forced into it or not, you'd rather be smooching. So would I."

"Let's just eat instead and stay out of trouble."

"Eat, then." He held a succulent morsel of honeyed lamb to her lips and lowered his voice to its huskiest. "Eat and stay out of trouble."

Trouble. It was there in his voice, in his devilish smile, right there at his fingertips. *Trouble.* She parted her lips and let him nudge the tidbit into her mouth. *Trouble.* She closed her lips around the tips of his fingers and heard him suck in a breath when her tongue made contact for a scintillating second.

It was as intimate as a mouth-to-mouth kiss and every bit as arousing. Rianna knew the last thing she should do was feed him a pinch of spiced rice in return, yet she did just that. Oh, the sensuous slide of his tongue between her first and middle fingers. Slowly she withdrew her hand. *Double trouble.*

"This is inviting it instead of staying out of it," she said.

Ty offered another tender morsel. "Tell me something I don't already know."

"Ty..."

"Open up," he urged softly. "Invite it."

Invite trouble? She should be shrinking from it, Rianna warned herself, even as she accepted his invitation. She shouldn't be opening, letting him feed her, trace the shape of her lips with his fingers, tell her with his eyes that he found her beautiful to behold. But she couldn't help it.

Taking up her wineglass, she took a sip and strove to recapture her composure. It did no good, for Ty's fingers sought hers on the stem of the glass and set the liquid in it trembling.

"It's insanity to act like lovers for no good reason," she told him.

"We have good reason," he said. "We're attracted to each other, and that's that."

She set down the wineglass and evaded his touch. "That isn't all there is to it. We have to go home together at some point tonight. If we keep tempting fate, we'll end up..."

"Making love?" he supplied after her moment of hesitation lengthened into two.

"We aren't in love, remember?"

"The urge I'm feeling is more than lust, Rianna. Relief is not all we want, though, is it?"

"Of course not."

"We want more. We're aching for it."

"We want too much too soon."

"It's not too soon for me, Rainbow. I'm more than ready for us to share something special tonight."

"I'm not sure I am yet, Ty."

"You're close." He leaned forward. "You should see your eyes right now. They're eating me alive. No, don't go shy on me again." He tipped up her chin with the middle knuckle of his forefinger. "Look at me, woman to man."

Woman to man she directed the heat of her gaze at him as he requested. Man to woman he returned it for long, emotion-packed seconds that only heightened the tension between them.

"When?" he murmured.

"Not tonight, Ty."

"When?"

"When it's right for both of us at the same time."

"Tonight is out?"

"It has to be. I don't know you well enough yet to sleep with you."

"You slept with me last night."

"Correction. *You* slept with *me*."

He nodded. "I behaved myself, too, if you recall. You're not the only one here with scruples."

"I'm the only one here," she gently pointed out, "who's talking sense right now."

"Only your mouth is talking sense. Your expression isn't. It's telling me what you feel, not what you think. You have the same definite and special feeling for me that I have for you. The better we know each other, the stronger it gets."

"Even so, will you promise you'll sleep in your own bed tonight?"

"Only if you promise in turn that I can read you to sleep first."

"I'll read *you* to sleep instead," she proposed. "How's that?"

"Fine, if I can choose the bedtime story," he responded.

"Nothing sexy, Ty."

"What? You don't trust yourself with the flower scene from *Lady Chatterley's Lover?*"

"You wouldn't."

"Try me." His smile was smug. "You have it on your bookshelf, way up high where most people don't notice it. I spied it today while you were painting."

"If that's your choice," said Rianna, "no one's getting read to sleep tonight."

"That's my choice."

"Forget I asked you to promise anything."

"Forget sleeping the night through, Rainbow."

LONG AFTER DINNER, alone in her bed, Rianna lay awake in the dark. The spring night outside was still and clear. Without a thick shroud of fog to muffle the sound, the breaking of the waves could be heard from the beach a half mile away. On such nights in the past, their rhythmic lapping had aided her in courting sleep.

On this night, however, the waves gave her no help. They only stirred up memories of walking on the beach with Ty the day before. She remembered how the sea breeze had ruffled his hair, recalled the support of his arm around her shoulders.

The fact that the pillow next to hers was the one Ty had slept on the night before didn't help, either. She had only to press her face into it to breathe in the masculine scent that lingered on the pillow slip. Since retiring to bed she had several times done just that, envisioning him holding her, making love to her, sleeping the night through with her. Now she was seriously considering joining him in the living room.

Was he sleeping? What would he think if she came to him in the night? Would he think her easy? Forward? Or simply straightforward? She thought back to the time when she had wanted to make love with Brent within a week of meeting him, yet had dated him three nights a week for two months before surrendering to her desire. Brent, on the other hand, had pressed hard from the first night for sexual intimacy.

"If you hadn't held out for a decent interval," he had confided to her after their engagement, "I'd have thought less of you. No man wants to marry an easy lay."

Rianna sighed. For all of the social and occupational parity women had gained in the past decade, they hadn't gained equal sexual ground. She wondered how many women would have thought Brent cheap for wanting to act out his desires from the word go.

Believing herself a savvy single woman of the nineties, Rianna knew the rules of the game hadn't changed much. And as far as a "decent interval" was concerned, she knew three days still didn't add up.

All of this boiled down to a thorny question. Why did she feel it so necessary that Ty should respect her? True, he talked a liberated line. Many men of the nineties did. Yet what they paid lip service to often wasn't what they believed deep in their hearts.

That still left her lying alone in the dark, wanting one thing, doing the opposite. And what was Ty doing in the next room? If he was still awake, the man wasn't arguing with himself whether three days was a decent interval or not.

THE NEXT DAY Rianna painted all morning after a short prebreakfast run with Ty, leaving him to work out on the Soloflex twice as long as he normally did with free weights at his gym.

After Ty's workout, Biff called in with the results of the license-plate search. He'd discovered that the car was registered to a rental company in Monterey. The man had rented it in the name of "John Hall" and had presented what Biff had determined was a bogus California driver's license.

"Want me to nab him on the phony ID?" Biff asked.

"No. Don't do anything until I figure out what he wants."

"You take care, Tyler T, and take even better care of the beautiful Miss Breece. There's a Class-A winner."

"I know one when I see one, too."

"Old man Breece'd bust a gut if he knew you were sleeping nights at her place, I expect."

"If 'John Hall' is his man, Breece knows by now."

"When do the fireworks start?"

"That's what I'm wondering."

"Know what I'm wondering?"

"What?"

"Why you sound like you're doing more than just bodyguarding the lady, good buddy."

"You need your ears examined, Biff."

"I've known you since sixth grade and it sounds to me like you're soft on her. You gonna get your heart busted up before you're through on this case?"

"Maybe."

"Her, too?"

"Maybe."

"Cryin' shame, if she's the one for you and you're the one for her. But hell, some things have a way of working out if two people want it bad enough."

"Not this thing."

"Like I said. Cryin' shame."

"I'll keep in touch, Biff."

"You do that."

Ty hung up and took his news to Rianna. "Our man's still a mystery," he told her. "He rented the car in Monterey under an alias."

"I'm not surprised," Rianna said. "Father's the type to cover his tracks."

Ty frowned. "Doesn't it seem odd to you that he hasn't called to rant and rave? I figured if our goon had reported our public behavior, you'd be hearing about it again by now."

Rianna shrugged. "He does have a news empire to run, you know."

Ty let it go at that. After lunch, he and Rianna walked into town to have his stitches removed by her doctor. That evening a gourmet pizza and a first-run film at the local movie theater rounded out the day. After a public afternoon of impulsive kisses on street corners and an evening of less conspicuous communing in the darkened cinema, Ty was glum when Rianna took to her bed alone immediately upon their return home.

"WOULD YOU MIND wearing those diamond studs while you're at it?" Ty called into the bedroom where Rianna had changed into a fuzzy pink sweater and black denim jeans before they left for dinner with the Gallaghers.

"Diamonds with jeans?" she called back dubiously.

"Why not?"

"Why for?"

"They'll taste great for dessert."

She wore them.

On the way to Gallaghers' in his black Acura Integra, Ty's attention was divided between her diamond-studded left ear, the beige sedan in the rearview mirror and the road ahead.

"He's keeping right up with us," Ty muttered and switched his glance from the rearview to Rianna's earlobe. "They do taste fantastic, you know. Especially after I warm them up."

Rianna almost squirmed in her seat. "Don't do it in front of six kids if you can help it."

"What if I can't help it? Knowing me, you shouldn't have worn them, especially at my request."

"You caught me in a weak moment."

"I wish I could catch you in more than a few more. I wonder how our friend back there would relish a moonlight stroll on the beach with us after dinner?"

Rianna resisted the temptation to look through the back window. "Do you think he knows we know he's following us?"

"That depends," said Ty.

"On what?"

"On whether he knows what my line of work is or not. If he's your father's man, he may just be following orders to follow *you*. If he's not..."

Rianna studied Ty's profile. "You never finish that sentence once you start it. What if he's not?"

"With your father keeping to himself for three days, I'm beginning to have doubts."

"What if he's not?" she persisted.

Her question went unanswered, for Ty steered at that moment into Biff and Jeannie Gallagher's driveway. The Acura had barely come to a stop when all six of the Gallagher children and two barking fox terriers came spilling through the front door of the remodeled sub-urban split-level.

Rianna estimated that the children's ages ranged from three to thirteen. Their parents followed them out and Rianna saw that the three boys and three girls had their plump mother's red hair and freckles and their tall, dark father's gray eyes.

Amid the noisy chorus of introductions Ty and Rianna were swept inside and made comfortable with wine in the family room.

"I hope you don't mind eating early," Jeannie said, blowing a fiery lock of hair off her forehead and smoothing her green corduroy tunic and pants. "This crowd has homework to do later."

"It's pasghetti for dinner tonight," sang three-year-old Kelsey with a lisp.

"Spaghetti," corrected five-year-old Sean.

"With meatballs," added seven-year-old Christina.

"And salad. Yuck," said nine-year-old Jordan.

"And garlic bread," chimed in eleven-year-old Sara.

"And spumoni ice cream for dessert," summed up thirteen-year-old Toby, who then proceeded to herd his antsy siblings off to another room to watch cartoon videos until dinner was served.

"How do you do it with six?" Rianna asked, regarding Jeannie and Biff with near awe.

"Easy." Jeannie chuckled. "Every night they set the table, clear the dishes, run the dishwasher and sweep the kitchen. It keeps us sane between laundry and grocery shopping and Scouts and soccer."

"Not to mention PTA, ballet and karate," said Biff, throwing a brawny arm around his wife's shoulders and giving her a hearty squeeze.

Rianna saw that they loved each other and were happy. It made her feel warm inside to look at them together.

Ty imitated his friend's gesture and clinked glasses with Rianna. "Didn't I tell you I have nice friends?"

"So you do, Ty," Jeannie agreed, regarding both him and Rianna with a knowing smile. "So you do."

They all seated themselves at the table when the children trooped back in. They were impressed and asked endless questions when they learned Rianna was an artist who painted animals—and *snakes!!!*

Dinner was delicious, and by the end Rianna was positive she had gained five pounds. She and Ty left soon after the spumoni. In the car she groaned as she clicked her seat belt into place. "I ate enough for two of me."

Ty laughed. "It's the quickest way to get invited back, I've found."

"Ah, so that's why you ate enough for three of you," she said dryly. "Where do you put it?"

He speared her with a suggestive glance. "Take a simple guess."

"We need a walk on the beach," Rianna suggested to divert him. "A long one, I think."

"Not tonight, on second thought. I don't want company like our friend tracking us down on a dark beach."

Rianna blew out a sigh. "That must mean he's still with us."

"Same car. Same goon," Ty confirmed.

"Which reminds me, Ty...what if he isn't my father's man?"

"Let's worry about that some other night." He looked at her. "You're safe with me. I guarantee it."

"Maybe I am, but my diamonds aren't," she teased with a toss of her head to make them glitter in the light from the dashboard. "However, you did eat two scoops of spumoni to take the edge off. Perhaps they're safe, after all."

"Are you flirting with me, Rianna?"

She took a quick look out the window. "A little."

"I like it," he said. "A lot. When we get home, I'll show you how much."

"I think we'd better watch TV or rent a movie instead, Ty."

"I'd rather read you to sleep and sleep with you."

They ended up bypassing the video shop and watching vintage episodes of *Twilight Zone* and *Perry Mason* on a cable network. At first she sat a good twelve inches away from Ty on the sofa. But by the time Mason had outwitted the district attorney and enjoyed the last laugh with Della Street, Rianna was somehow snuggled up against Ty, his arm around her, her head on his shoulder.

"Bedtime for the boob tube," he said and sighed, punching the Off button on the remote control with one hand, while the other toyed with a button on the shoulder of Rianna's pink sweater. "You sleepy, Rainbow?"

"No."

"Have a good time tonight?"

"Wonderful."

"Still too full of 'pasghetti'?"

"No. Just right."

"Happy?"

She tilted her head to look at him. "Very."

"Me, too. I've felt happier by the minute ever since I met you." He slid a fingertip under her chin and tilted it higher. "I'm beginning to hope your father flies by way of the North Pole to have his heart-to-heart with you."

"He'll fly due south by the weekend," Rianna assured Ty. "You should have heard him on the phone when he called."

"That doesn't give us much time."

"For what?"

"For this," Ty murmured, touching his lips to hers. "And more." He drew back and looked at her. "I want to make love with you. Tonight."

She closed her eyes and swallowed hard. "I know you do."

"What do *you* want, Rainbow?"

"The same thing." She opened her eyes. "I wish I didn't, Ty. I wish I didn't care about you enough to want you."

"It's enough that we *both* care," he soothed her. "I wish we had more time, too. But we don't. How long before our little bubble bursts with a family feud? Two days? Three?"

"Something like that—if we keep necking in public." She could barely get the words out with Ty's seductive mouth hovering a whisper away.

"Let's make the most of the time we have, Rianna." He pressed soft kisses to her brow, her eyelids, her cheekbones.

"Yes, Ty."

He pulled back, surprised. "Did you say yes, or am I hearing things?"

She touched her lips to his. "I said yes."

"Tonight?"

"Tonight."

"All *right,*" he whispered into her ear, before tasting her earlobe and the tiny diamond there. He tasted again with a slow, circular stroke and Rianna was lost.

At the long sigh of surrender she released, Ty skimmed his mouth from her ear across the softness of her cheek and found her lips ripe and trembling, eager for his.

It was far from their first kiss, but the meeting of their mouths was so passionate, so hungry, so devouring of every available sensation that it might have been their first.

As always when he kissed her, Rianna was immediately aroused as Ty's tongue silkily plundered her lips. It blotted everything else out, and she never knew how he eventually came to be lying against her, crushing her into the soft pillows, one thigh wedged between hers. Not until he moaned and broke the kiss did she realize how lost in him she had been.

With that came certainty; this night would be one to remember and treasure in her heart forever, whatever might happen afterward. She had known sexual satisfaction in Brent Halston's arms, but had never lost herself in his kisses as she had been doing for days in Ty's.

"We're going to go wild tonight," Ty breathed against her throat; his hand slid under her sweater. He committed to memory every curve, every nuance of Rianna's high, firm breasts and hard nipples. "Little by little, my beautiful Rainbow, we're going to go out of our minds with each other."

He wanted her hand on his, wanted her fingers to ride his as he stroked her to fullness and made her whimper with pleasure. The fingers of her free hand, though, were occupied under *his* sweater, tracing the muscles he had honed and conditioned that day, whisking his flat nipples to pebbled points until he was breathing hard and fast.

He shifted and drew her sweater over her head, pulled off his own, then settled down and held her against his chest, nipple to nipple.

"Any qualms?" he whispered.

"No," she lied. "And you?"

"None. I know from the supply of birth-control pills in your medicine chest that we won't be making babies tonight."

"I . . . never stopped taking them after Brent. I hope that doesn't make you think I—"

He pressed a silencing finger to her lips. "It makes me think you hoped you'd meet someone like me. I don't sleep around, either, but I'm always prepared." He grinned and added, "Just in case I fall halfway in love when I least expect it."

His frank acknowledgment of his own preparedness and acceptance of her own encouraged her. After a moment of hesitation she confessed, "Ty, I do have a qualm."

"What?"

"It's embarrassing."

When she still hesitated, he said, "You can tell me."

"I'm..." She bit her lip. "I'm...I need more time than most women. Brent always said I took too long. Someone else did, too. Before Brent. There. Now you know the worst."

"I'd call it knowing the best. A man can go crazy wondering if a woman's faking or not. I'm glad I won't have to wonder with you."

"I try, Ty. It just doesn't come easy for me."

He slipped his hands from her back to her breasts and cherished her nipples with the pads of his thumbs. "You don't have to try for me, Rainbow. The more foreplay the better, as far as I'm concerned. I don't care if you take all night as long as you enjoy every minute of what we do together."

Rianna shut her eyes and let out her breath in a long sigh of relief. She felt Ty's palms cover her and let the pleasure of his touch lead her from thinking to feeling.

"Tyler Toranaga," she murmured, "you're marvelous!"

"I get even better as I go along." He lowered his mouth and kissed circles around each of her breasts. When he came to each pink, swollen nipple, he took it between his teeth and lashed his tongue over it before drawing it into his mouth to suck. Again and again he repeated the gestures of love until Rianna clasped his thigh between her own and began a rocking pelvic motion against him.

Furling his tongue back into the sweetness of her mouth, he glided his open hand between his thigh and the delta of her jeans to palm her soft mound. Breathing into her mouth as he squeezed and kneaded, he whispered that he'd please her in any way she liked. Anything, he told her, anything she wanted he was hot to do.

She felt wilder by the second, raking her hands through his black hair, over his back, his chest. His nipples responded as readily as hers had to the stimulus of a wet mouth and restless tongue. She grew wilder still when he guided her seeking hand between his jeans and silk boxers and told her she could do anything she wanted.

Never had a man ravished her with words as Ty then proceeded to do. They rolled off his tongue, sugarcoated one moment, shameless the next. He whispered them into her ears and her mouth and breathed them all over her breasts. Never had a man said such things to her, drawn her stroking hand out of his pants and kissed her fingertips in silent gratitude for her intimate caress, or swung her into his arms and carried her into a bedroom. Ty did.

And when he laid her tenderly on her bed and stripped off her shoes, jeans and panties, she knew a greater need for him than she had ever known for a man. Her hands were more than ready to rid him of his jeans and socks after he kicked off his shoes. Only when it came to drawing down his black silk boxers did she falter.

"I'll take care," he whispered, lying down next to her. "I won't hurt you." He surveyed her body and ran one hand over her breasts, then let it drift palm down to the pale cloud of curls between her thighs. Gently he wove the tip of his middle finger into that cloud and sought the hidden, perfect spot.

"You're as wet as I am hard, Rainbow," he whispered, curving that deft finger inward to assay her response. "You're ready."

Rianna moaned as he began to stroke the bud of her pleasure with the dew of her desire. "It's never happened so soon before. I don't understand it."

"I do. You never trusted your man before. Not completely. That makes me feel pretty special, Rainbow."

"You're superspecial, Ty. You know where and how to touch me. Everything you do I love."

"Anything you don't love, just tell me." He shifted position to settle between her legs and taste his way from her nipples to the rim of her navel. "More, angel?"

"Yes. . . ."

He dipped his tongue into her navel. "More?"

"Ty..." Rianna framed his face in her hands. "When do I get to please *you* in every way?"

He skimmed his lips to the point where the first pale tendrils of her maiden hair began. "Later. I couldn't take it right now."

"Later, then," she agreed, her eyes falling shut as he stroked her again with his fingertips, just where she was most sensitive. "Oh, Ty... that feels too good to be believed."

"More? Tell me, Rainbow."

"More."

"My mouth, too?"

"Oh, yes. Yes."

He kissed every inch of her inner thighs from the knees inward, stopping just short of her center. Between kisses he told her how beautiful he found her secret place, how sexy, luscious and tempting. Then he touched his mouth to her, opened her up, parted her with the tip of his tongue.

Rianna panted and shivered. She snaked her hands along his arms, then cried out for more as he brought her close, so close to total abandon.

He slid up, his lips ruddy and glistening, his eyes devouring hers. There, where his tongue had already loved her, he pressed the plum-smooth tip of his sex.

Rianna reached out and led him into her. Halfway in, he drew her hands toward the pillow under her head and clasped them in his own.

"Ah, Rainbow," he rasped. "Look into my eyes as I go in." He sank himself deeper into her, then kissed her to seal their union.

Rianna began to crest before he completed his second long downstroke. "Ty!" she gasped. "I'm going to . . . oh . . . oh . . . I'm . . ." Her eyes widened.

"Yes," he urged, short-stroking her to bliss. "Burn up all around me."

She shuddered into her first spasm with another gasp, into the second with a cry, and the third with a near scream. Through each succeeding one she was able only to cling to Ty and chant his name until the height of her pleasure had been reached.

Ty watched joy suffuse her face, felt her hands clutch his flexing hips, saw her flush deep pink from her breasts up when she lost herself to him and heard her ecstatic repetition of his name. Then, when his final, deepest thrust touched the roots of Rianna's womb, he let all that he had held back for that moment flood into her.

Rianna felt his release as a molten surge that carried them away to a place where incoherent cries gradually gave way to soft moans and murmurs of amazement.

"Tell me I never have to move," Ty finally whispered a long time later into the curve of Rianna's shoulder.

Rianna tightened the grip of her legs around his hips and possessively clasped her arms around his back. "You never have to move. I won't let you go."

Ty braced himself on his hands and looked down; they were still joined, Rianna's pale curls laced into the black hair at his groin. He studied her breasts, whose nipples were soft, sated and pink, and pressed a cherishing kiss upon both. "I've never felt the oneness I feel," he said. "Not until now with you."

"Me too. Until now I thought it was a myth."

"Staggers the mind, doesn't it?"

She nodded. "And the body."

"And the heart." Ty pressed a second kiss upon her left breast. "And the soul." He kissed her lips. "What we have here is more than a fleeting thing, Rainbow. What we have here is . . ."

"Don't say it, Ty," Rianna warned him softly.

"We already said it without words," he murmured, nuzzling her nipples. "We can't take it back. We're falling."

"Ty, we might be falling, but—"

"Not might," he cut in. "We are. Fast."

"Too fast," she cautioned. "We can't fall all the way."

"What's to stop us now that we're both out of control?" he inquired, rolling onto his back and holding her straddled over his hips. "Tell me, Rainbow."

"We're not out of control," she said, unconvinced by her own words.

"I am. I can't stop getting hard again right now." He rolled his fingertips over her nipples and watched them stiffen. "Neither can you."

"I can't believe it, Ty. I've never, ever been this way before."

"Out of control, you mean?"

She couldn't deny it. Heart, mind, body and soul, she was in control of nothing.

"Yes. Do you mind?" she inquired with a sigh before she touched the thumb of her right hand to his left nipple and lowered her open mouth to the other.

"God, no." Ty arched his hips and furrowed her hair with his fingers, implicitly encouraging her to continue.

"You taste fantastic," she murmured against his skin. "You feel fantastic." She grazed his nipples with her teeth and thumbnail and felt him shudder beneath her. "I want you on my terms this time, Ty."

"Take me. Make me yours, Rainbow mine."

9

RIANNA WOKE LATE the next morning, lying on her side with Ty curled behind her, holding her as if she were his most treasured possession. When she stirred and snuggled her bottom deeper into the curve of his body, he tightened his embrace. It was heaven to wake like this. Even more heavenly was feeling as cherished and protected and cared for as she did in Ty's strong arms.

She touched his hand where it cupped her breast and thought back over the night they had spent together. Never had she known a night like it or a lover like Ty. More than once he had taken her with tender patience, more than once with raw, searing passion.

She hadn't thought herself capable of some of the things she had done with him. Now, having been utterly open and outrageous with him, she thrilled at the thought of being that way again . . . soon.

"Ty?" she whispered as he stirred behind her.

"Hmm?"

"Nothing. . . . Wondering if you were awake."

He gathered her closer and slid his hand from her breast to nestle it between her thighs. "It's heaven to wake up like this, Rainbow."

"How do you do that?"

"What?" he murmured.

"Say exactly what I'm thinking."

"Easy. We think alike." He fanned her nipple with his thumb. "Know what *I'm* thinking?"

"I think so. We're going to stay in bed all day."

"Bingo. Just like honeymooners."

Rianna parted her thighs to welcome the downward drift of his caress. "What about your room at La Playa? Who's going to mess it up for us?"

"Us. That's where we're going to stay in bed all day after we have breakfast."

"I'll never get out of the bed we're in if you keep making me want to stay, Ty."

"Am I making you want to?"

"You know what you're doing."

"Do I ever. And I *like* it," he said, moving his hips against her bottom as his fingers found their knowing way to her sweet, secret spot and set about making it swell with pleasure. "Do you like it, too?"

"No. I *love* it."

"Shameless hussy," he whispered into the curve of her shoulder. "What else do you love? Say it and you'll have it."

"Every inch of you inside me."

"Where did you say you want me, Rainbow?"

"Right where you belong."

He obliged by holding her derriere firmly against his belly and thrusting partway in. "Oh, Lord," he groaned, "what you do to me. After last night I should be half-dead instead of harder than ever."

"More, Ty," Rianna urged. "Now. Every inch of you."

Afterward they showered together and had brunch, so it was afternoon when they drove rather than walked the few blocks to La Playa in Ty's car. Following at a discreet distance was the beige sedan.

Once in the room, Rianna flopped onto the bed. "Privacy!" she exclaimed with a sigh. "At last. Again."

Ty walked to the window and gazed out distractedly for several moments.

"What's wrong, Ty?"

He shrugged and came to lie down next to her. "I'm not sure. Maybe nothing. Then again . . ."

"What?"

"It still seems odd that your father hasn't made much of a scene yet."

"He will. Don't worry."

"The way we've been all over each other all over town, I thought he'd be down here on the double."

"Ty, he's a busy man who's never been able to delegate half of what he should. He'll be here by the weekend to dress me down. You can depend on it."

Ty drew her into his arms and murmured, "Speaking of dressing down, let's dress down to nothing and unmake this bed."

"We could do that," Rianna instantly agreed and began to unbutton his shirt.

"You're glowing, Rainbow."

"What I should be doing is blushing to my roots. I can't imagine what you think of me."

"I think you're beautiful."

She disposed of the last button on his shirt and moved lower. "What else do you think? A few days ago I didn't even know your name. Now look at me."

"I think you're the most fantastic woman I've ever met."

"Even though I'm unbuckling your belt?"

"You can stop blushing," he advised. "I think you're the most beautiful, fantastic woman I've ever respected in my life. And the sexiest, too."

She drew down his zipper. "I've never been this sexy."

"Not even when you were engaged?"

"Never. I've never wanted any man the way I want you. I've never been the way I am in bed with you."

He raised an eyebrow as she spread open the V of his pants fly and drew him out through the slit in his black silk boxers. "To be perfectly honest, you're the only woman I've ever been up twenty-four hours straight for," he confided in turn, mesmerized by the strokes of her fingers on the smooth shaft of his penis.

"Ty, you're so exciting!" she whispered, bending to touch her open lips to him and then the flat of her tongue. "Tell me what you like . . . what you want . . ."

He never had to say a word, for Rianna returned her mouth to him and instinctively began doing everything he liked, everything he wanted or could have asked of her. Somewhere in the delicious space of that long afternoon, Ty made a decision. Whatever the odds, he vowed, he wanted Rianna Whitney Breece in his life for good. If he could swing it, he would.

THAT EVENING they had dinner sent up to the room and dined in bed. They did the same with breakfast the following morning. Not until afternoon did they emerge from their intimate cocoon for a romantic walk on the beach before returning to the cottage and another unforgettable night.

"I love you, Rainbow," Ty solemnly told her when they woke again in each other's arms.

"I love you, too," she replied—and burst into tears.

Ty held her and soothed, "Don't cry. It's not the end of the world to be in love."

"It is for us. We have no future to look forward to," she sobbed.

"I've been thinking we could have one if we really wanted it," he ventured with due caution. "It wouldn't be the first time either of us walked against a stiff wind."

"I'm Nathan Breece's only child, Ty. In every major way but one I've disappointed him. That's enough in itself for a man whose heart has already been broken by Uncle Ned's death and Mother's suicide. If I married you, it would be the last straw. Your parents would disown you, too, wouldn't they?"

"I'd have to confront them and stand my ground. They wouldn't be happy about it, but if you and I got as far as the altar, they'd put a good face on things for my sake."

"Father wouldn't."

"Maybe you're underestimating him. After all, he hasn't flown down to shake his fist at you yet. He hasn't even called again."

No sooner had Ty spoken than the phone rang, startling both of them into tense silence. Ty placed one hand upon the receiver and raised his eyebrows. She wiped her eyes and shook her head.

"Maybe it's time I had a man-to-man with him," Ty said.

Rianna shook her head again. "Things are upsetting enough as it is. Let it ring."

He couldn't. He picked it up. "Hello? Oh, hi, Ruby."

Rianna slumped back into the pillows and dabbed at her wet cheeks with a corner of the sheet, relieved that it was Ty's secretary calling and not her father. However, after seeing Ty's expression become tensely alert as Ruby spoke, Rianna sat up again.

"What is it?" she demanded the minute he finished listening and hung up.

"The drug lord's been nabbed. His alibi for the day Al was killed is full of holes. The addict who testified against him has suddenly disappeared. He's not denying that he made her disappear." Ty's dark brows rushed together. "I had one of my men tailing her, but he lost the track two days ago. Now she's nowhere to be found. Seems she was the one that note referred to. Not you."

"Note?"

"The one that warned, 'Lay off or she's next.'"

Rianna thought back to the night Ty had told her of the note and Al's death. "I thought it said, 'Lay off or else.'"

"I fibbed on the last half of it. I didn't want to scare you." He brushed a tear from her cheek.

"I'm not the 'she' who was next, then?"

"It looks that way."

"What happens now?"

"One of two things. I go back to San Francisco and help pry a confession out of Al's murderer, or..."

"That's one," she prodded as he hesitated. "What's the other?"

"I stay here until your father shows and *then* go back to San Francisco." Ty chewed the inside of his cheek. "I wish I knew for sure that he hired our friend with the phony driver's license."

The phone rang again and when Ty moved to answer it, Rianna stopped him. "My turn to play telephone roulette," she said, leaning over him and taking up the receiver.

"Hello?"

"When are you going to stop seeing that...?" Nathan Breece growled at the other end.

Her stomach coiled. "Hello, Father. It's nice to chat with you again, too."

"I didn't call to shoot the breeze. When is your fling with Toranaga going to stop?"

"How do you know it hasn't?"

"Carmel Beach has eyes. They saw both of you there yesterday. What do I have to do? Fly down in person to shake some sense into you?"

"Be reasonable and let me live my adult life as I see fit."

"He's not fit for you."

"He's more fit for me than any man I've ever known."

"Blast it! I *will* fly down, by God, if you don't straighten up!"

"You're shouting again."

"I'm having chest pains again, too!"

"You have chest pains because you're yelling."

"I never yell!"

"You're breaking my eardrum, Father. Goodbye for now."

"Don't you dare hang up that phone, young lady! I won't have it, do you hear? I won't—"

Rianna handed the squawking receiver to Ty. "There's all the proof you can possibly want," she told him. "Carmel Beach, he swears, has eyes that spotted us yesterday. He should know. He hired those eyes to spy on us."

"That's that, then, I guess," Ty said after a short, bleak silence. "He'll stop having chest pains when his spy tells him I'm headed back to the city, where I belong."

Rianna moved into the arms Ty held out for her. "When do you plan to head back?" she mumbled against his chest.

"Tomorrow. I want to wake up just one more morning with you before I leave." He buried his lips in her hair and held her tight. "I'll take off after breakfast tomorrow."

"This isn't how I pictured it ending, Ty. It's so sudden."

He nodded. "I thought we'd have more time, too. Maybe it's best this way. We won't fall any deeper in love than we already are."

"I never meant to fall," she said.

"I didn't, either."

"I've fallen hard, Ty."

"Me, too." He stared over her head at the rainbow mural on the opposite wall. "I wish there was something we could do about it."

"There's nothing to do."

"There's one thing," Ty mused, attempting a smile.

She pulled back and looked at him. "What?"

"The obvious. We can do what we've been doing until we think of something better."

Rianna couldn't help smiling back through her tears. "What we've been doing is making love like there's no tomorrow."

"All the more reason to enjoy today," said Ty, kissing her tears away. "Let's make this last one our finest, Rainbow. The best we've ever had."

AS TY HAD PROPOSED, their last full day together was their best, if bittersweet. Stopping now and then to hold each other and kiss for long moments, they walked the white sands of Carmel Beach. Then south to Nepenthe they drove for cheese, fruit and wine on the sunny terrace overlooking the rugged Big Sur coastline. On the way back to Carmel, they stopped at Point Lobos State Reserve and watched sea otters feed on shellfish.

Their champagne dinner for two at the Casanova was delectable and romantic. Later they danced to classic tunes at the Jazz Age nightclub.

Leaving the club, they meandered into a novelty shop that stayed open late. There Ty bought Rianna a pair of enamel earrings shaped and colored to resemble tiny rainbows. "To remember me by," he told her, slipping the little box that contained them into her coat pocket.

Later in the cottage Ty slowly undressed her in the soft glow of candlelight. "Now," he said, "you have more than a rainbow a day to wish on if you want."

"Thank you, Ty," she whispered, touching the rainbows in her ears, "for everything."

"My pleasure," he returned, lowering her silk dress to the floor, then her lace slip, matching bra and panties.

Rianna stepped out of the silky pile and drew Ty, whom she had already undressed with the same tender care, onto the bed. He touched his tongue to one exquisite enamel rainbow, then the other.

"You have these to remember me by," he murmured, "but what am I going to remember you by, Rainbow?"

"You already have something, Ty."

He knelt over her, memorizing every line and curve of her face with his lips and hands. "Yes, I have turquoise eyes to remember. There aren't another two like them anywhere else." He kissed her. "No lips are as soft and ripe as yours." He slipped his tongue between her teeth. "No mouth is as sweet." He kissed the slope of her throat, sucked her pink nipples to dark rose peaks, then drew back to gaze at her. "Why do I always feel as if I knew every detail on your body before I ever laid eyes on you?"

"Because you knew me before you knew me," Rianna confessed. "I've known it since that first night."

A slight frown puckered his brow. "What night? What are you talking about?"

"The night we had dinner at La Playa when you said you owned Nordstrom's *Hope.* I didn't know how to tell you until now."

"Tell me what?"

"I posed for Eric as a favor when he was too poor to pay a model. My only condition was that he leave the facial features on the figure indistinct to protect my identity."

Ty pulled back a little, stunned. Then recognition dawned. "You're . . . *Hope?*"

"Yes. I was yours in bronze long before we met. You have something very special to remember me by."

Ty pulled back further. "I just can't . . . you posing nude for him . . ."

"Eric and I were never lovers," she said, anticipating his next thought. "I posed. That's all, I swear."

Ty sank beside her with a sigh. "This is incredible. You don't know how many times *Hope*—you—came alive in my wildest dreams." He swept a hand over her breasts and belly. "But never alive to me like this." He drew her into his arms. "Never like this."

"Promise you'll never sell her to anyone else," she whispered, melting into his embrace. "No matter what."

Ty kissed her brows, her eyelids, her cheeks, her lips. "Never," he promised fervently. "She's mine as long as I live."

"MARRY ME, Rianna."

"I can't," she said as he knew she would.

"We'd have beautiful children."

"I know we would."

"I could work out of Monterey if you want to stay here. We'd need a bigger house, though, for a family."

"Ty, don't."

"Would you if you could?"

"Yes. I'd marry you and take your name and have babies and grow old and gray with you."

"Marry me, then. My parents will come around to accepting you in time."

"Father will never come around. It would kill him, Ty."

"What about me? I love you. I want to make love with you for the rest of my life."

"Make love to me now. Again."

"Is that the most you'll say yes to?"

"Yes."

He touched his mouth to her breast. "Yes to this?"

"Yes."

"And this?"

"Oh, yes."

"And . . . this?"

"Ahh, yes . . ."

IT WAS RAINING the next morning when Ty packed his things into the trunk of his coupe and drove off. From the front gate, where she had kissed the love of her life for the last time, Rianna saw the beige sedan pull away from the curb and follow Ty's car out of sight.

Ten minutes later she lay huddled in bed crying her heart out. The doorbell rang. *Ty?* She threw on a red fleece robe. The bell rang again. *He must have forgotten something.* She blew her nose and hurried to the door, checking the peephole before opening up.

Instead of Ty's smooth face, she saw a wrinkled, ruddy one, an unruly shock of blue-white hair, eyes the same deep turquoise as her own. Nathan Breece. Behind him at the curb was a long, white limousine.

Oh, Lord. Just what she needed right now. Her only consolation was that she could tell her father with a clear conscience that Ty Toranaga was history.

"Where is he?" were the first words the older man growled when she opened the door.

"Gone."

"For good?"

"Yes."

"Good, then. May I come in and give my only daughter a fatherly kiss and hug?"

"Yes, Father."

He stepped in and Rianna went willingly into his arms for the customary bear hug and hearty kiss on both cheeks. He wore his usual navy flannel Savile Row suit, pale blue shirt and Harvard tie. Rianna hadn't expected to, but felt oddly comforted by her father's stocky, solid presence and the fact that he really did love her more than anything in the world.

As always when he released her, he looked around, grimaced at the rainbows on the walls and shook his head. "Why you and Gordo can't live in normal houses like your parents before you is beyond me," he said.

Rianna thought of his Manhattan town house and the Nob Hill mansion, not to mention the summer house; she almost choked. And Mame had two grand homes, yet not one of them could be called "normal."

"Less for me is more," she said, motioning him to the sofa where she joined him. "Gordo agrees. Would you like a cup of coffee or tea?"

"No, thank you. I just dropped by to see how you are."

"And to pound some sense into me about Tyler Toranaga," Rianna added, on the verge of tears as she spoke his name.

"Yes. As you well know. You've been crying, I see. Over him?"

"What does it matter?" She sniffed back a wave of tears. "It's over." She swallowed hard. "He's gone back to S-S-San—" Her chin quivered, and she struggled to get Ty's destination out. She felt her eyes fill and the tears spill over. Two seconds later she was weeping all over the front of her father's suit coat.

"Now, Rianna, it's all for the best," he said, awkwardly patting her shoulder, clearly as unnerved by the flood as any man of his age and generation could be. He pulled a handkerchief from his breast pocket and dabbed ineffectually at her cheeks. "It's all for the best, now," he muttered. "He's not our kind. Never will be."

"He's my kind. I love him, Father," Rianna sobbed, taking the handkerchief and blowing her nose before the next wave of tears overtook her.

"No self-respecting Breece loves a Jap," Nathan grunted.

"I do." Rianna wept into the handkerchief.

"You can't. Remember what they did to Ned?" His voice broke on the name. "The finest big brother a man could love, and they strafed him down on the deck of his battleship." Nathan Breece shook his head. "No, Rianna. You only think you love him."

By now Rianna was crying too hard to get any words out whole.

"Chin up, now," her father soothed. "This isn't the brave daughter I saw holding her head high and her tears dry after Brent Halston did his dirty work. That bastard."

"You thought he was suitable for me."

"Not until he signed the ironclad prenuptial agreement I insisted on. After that I gave him the benefit of the doubt. Before he signed, he was just another millionaire wanting to be a billionaire. Turned out I had him pegged right in the first place. He lost his million in the crash and didn't want to work his way back to six figures."

The great debt she owed her overbearing father over that prenuptial agreement, one he'd had to force her into and which had ultimately exposed Brent's rotten core, was nothing she wanted to be reminded of at that moment.

"You faced facts then," Nathan Breece continued. "Face them now."

Rianna summoned back her lost control and straightened her spine. "I already did, Father. Last night I told Ty I could never, ever marry him."

Nathan stared at her, horrified. "He asked you to *marry* him!"

"Yes. He asked me, even though your editorials still support the government policy that put his parents behind barbed wire for most of the war. Even though those loyal American citizens lost everything they owned because of racists like Grandfather and you, he asked me to marry him and be the mother of his children."

Her father scowled, stood and moved to the door. "You'll be glad you refused. One day you'll thank me."

Rianna followed him, anticipating the philosophic quote he always came up with after securing the last word in any argument.

"Time heals all wounds," he said, stepping outside.

When she responded, her tone was firm. "Not your wounds, Father. Mine, perhaps, but never yours."

She watched him open his mouth to refute her, then close it. That and a sudden, visible slump of his shoulders told her the words had hit home. Powerful though he was, he was unable to defend himself against the truth in her reply.

When he hugged her goodbye, she felt him tremble slightly. But as he passed through the gate to his chauffeured limousine, she saw his shoulders straighten again, his step grow lighter with renewed confidence.

Rianna shut the door. Nothing short of a miracle, she knew, would change the mind Nathan Breece had made up about Tyler Toranaga.

10

FORTY-EIGHT HOURS after kissing Rianna for the last time, Ty was mired in frustration. He hadn't slept for two nights, wanting Rianna, yet knowing he couldn't have her. Time and again in those dark hours he'd picked up the phone to call her, then replaced it before dialing her number. He knew he had to get over her. God, it was worse than any hurt he'd ever known.

The past two days had been pure frustration on all other counts, too. The drug lord had clammed up under questioning about Al's murder and the addict's disappearance. Neither Ty nor the police had been able to get a word out of him so far. With his whereabouts on the day of the murder still in question, with no answers after two days of interrogation, the murder investigation was up against a brick wall.

Faced with that and the hell of life without Rianna, Ty might have been literally climbing the walls of his office if a call hadn't come from an informant in Monterey to report that Crayton Thorn's yacht had docked there just before noon. Rumor had it that the boat would rendezvous with another to receive a shipment of rare birds and Australian reptile skins. The meeting was supposed to take place in a hidden cove on the coast near Big Sur just before dawn the next morning.

More desperate for action then he'd ever been, Ty rented a car, as his own was in for repairs, and drove down to Monterey late that night. With only that rumor to go on, he thought it better not to inform the coast guard or the feds. The most he hoped to do was stake out the cove and photograph the rendezvous. With evidence like that, the feds could then undertake a full investigation.

After a midnight meeting with his informant, Ty stationed himself alone, well before dawn, on a rock outcropping overlooking the cove. He stared through the darkness and recalled the day when he'd gazed in the same westerly direction and witnessed a double rainbow. He thought of the earrings he'd given her and wondered if she was wearing them in bed. Or was she painting in her studio at that moment, battling insomnia again? He remembered the night she had painted fog, when they had wept together for those they would never see again.

He'd been attracted to her from the very second her name had come up in the smuggling case. He remembered snapping shut the file marked Rianna Breece after a long study of the arresting photo it contained and assigning the case to Al, so that his own involvement would be as minimal as possible. His reaction to that photo had been inexplicable, intense and deeply disturbing.

Yes, he'd been attracted to her long before that first night. He still remembered the secret sigh of relief he'd breathed when Al had called to say he was convinced she was clean. There had been something about her that reached out to something in him from the outset.

A sudden, biting gust of wind from the sea roused him from his thoughts. He stood up and stretched his legs, wishing he was with Rianna in her warm bed instead of freezing his ass off on a stakeout. He pulled the hood of his heavy quilted parka over the navy knit watch cap he wore, then a stronger gust of wind sent him in search of shelter.

Damn, it was cold. And getting colder. He checked the illuminated digits of his wristwatch. One hour left before the first light of dawn. He closed his eyes against the stinging wind and tried not to think anymore of the warmth of Rianna's bed and the memory of her beautiful body in his arms.

He ached to love her as he had so many times before the end. Thinking back, he wasn't sure which of them had been the more awestruck. Rianna, perhaps, because her need of a partner generous with foreplay had never been met before. She had always thought it *her* problem, not attributing her difficulty to her lover's selfishness or lack of skill.

Ty tried to console himself with the recognition that, if nothing else had come of their brief relationship, Rianna would know forevermore what she deserved from a lover in bed. But there was no consolation for him in knowing that he had never been as compatible with any woman as he had with her. It was too much to expect it would happen again with someone else.

Knowing and understanding Rianna's reasons for ending the relationship only made things worse. After all, he couldn't swear he wouldn't have made the same decision if they'd switched places.

He opened his eyes. Here he was, freezing, miserable, weary, and getting nowhere with getting over Rianna Whitney Breece. The wind had dropped, and a thick fog was rolling in from the ocean. He could feel the heavy wet of it on his face. Holding his wristwatch an arm's length away, he could see that visibility was being reduced to a few feet. At this rate, two yachts could rendezvous right under his nose and he'd never get a single incriminating frame onto film.

And indeed he heard the approach of an engine-powered vessel a few minutes later. The motor stopped. Another couple of seconds and there came the sound of another vessel. Ty heard a shout, then silence.

They were insane, Ty thought, to attempt a cargo transfer in this pea soup. He couldn't even make out the green-lit digits of his watch anymore. Visibility was two feet at best.

MIDMORNING found him staring glumly through a coffee-shop window at the empty slip that the pleasure yacht *Thorn's Way* had occupied in Monterey harbor before sailing up the coast in the hours before dawn.

After spending several futile hours waiting for the impenetrable fog to lift, Ty had returned to Monterey, fully expecting to see the yacht back in dock. But he'd found the slip still empty.

Craving sleep now in the worst way, Ty hunched over the café counter and his third thick mugful of the worst dockside coffee he'd ever drunk.

He glanced out again at the slip and started; *Thorn's Way* was approaching, nosing its way in. He took a sharp breath and watched Crayton Thorn himself and a deckhand secure the lines. Their task completed, both disappeared below deck.

The waitress behind the counter yanked a coffeepot off its burner and offered him yet another cup of black poison. As she poured, she drawled, "You been done wrong?"

"Everyone's been done wrong sometime or other," Ty replied, keeping one eye on *Thorn's Way.*

"You're tellin' me? Look at the proof I got here." She gestured down the counter, which was full of scruffy men, who all appeared to be nursing hangovers. "All been done wrong to hear *them* tell it. What's *your* sob story?"

Ty shrugged. "She was too good for me."

"Well, there's a new one," she claimed, looking taken aback for a beat. "You're the first one I ever heard admit he done *her* wrong.

"No wonder you're torchin' for her." The waitress nodded knowingly, looking him over again with a kinder, gentler eye. "Musta just happened, eh?"

Ty drained his cup and handed her a twenty-dollar bill. "I'm not on the skids yet, if that's what you mean," he said with a wry smile. "Answer me a question or two and you can keep the change."

She fingered the bill and gave him a suspicious frown. "You a cop, by any chance?"

"Me a cop?" He tried to look as incredulous and insulted as he'd ever looked in his life.

"Just checkin'. Pop me a question." She folded the bill and pocketed it.

He glanced out the window at *Thorn's Way*. "A pal of mine mentioned that cruiser might need extra crew. Anyone ever come in here from that one?"

"The big snazzeroo? A coupla deckhands with a taste for greasy burgers came in yesterday."

"You wouldn't know where she's bound from here, would you?"

"Back to Frisco one of 'em said. The Giants fan in the baseball hat was the one in the know."

Years of undercover surprises kept Ty from moving a telltale muscle. "Giants fan?" He forced himself to bait her with the wrong question, hoping to hook the right answer and keep himself looking the total innocent. "Little skinny guy, by any chance?"

"No way. Big bruiser with a beer gut." She pointed out the window. "That's him now."

He followed her pointing finger and saw a familiar, beefy figure wearing a baseball cap disembark from the yacht. In his hand the big man carried what looked like a rolled-up beach towel. As nonchalantly as he could, Ty took up his parka and slid off his stool. "I think I'll just mosey out and scout up a crew job for myself."

"Talk hits and runs and you can't miss," the waitress advised. She patted her pocket. "Thanks for the tip."

"Keep it to yourself. Have a good one."

"You, too. Hey, don't eat your heart out!" she called after him.

Once outside, Ty fished his knit watch cap and a pair of mirrored sunglasses out of his parka pocket. He pulled the cap down to his eyebrows and the cotton turtleneck he wore under his sweater up to his chin. With the sunglasses on and his parka slung over one shoulder, he shadowed the man in the baseball cap.

Never assume anything! How many times had it been drilled into him as a cop? How many times had he drilled it into a green rookie? With every step he took, Ty grimly berated himself for his assumption that the goon had been hired by Nathan Breece, even though everything had pointed in that direction the day he left for San Francisco.

Was Rianna safe? Ty remembered that the beige sedan had followed him to the city. He had assumed that the man was simply making certain his quarry had returned there for good.

Ready to strangle himself for his own stupidity, Ty watched his prey go into a bait and tackle shop. Across the street was a phone booth. Keeping his eye on the shop door, Ty dialed Rianna's number. No answer. *Dear God, is she safe?* He dialed Carmel police headquarters. *A busy signal!* He dialed his office and got an immediate answer—along with an update from Ruby that left him stunned.

The murder investigation had gone bust, Ruby told him. Los Angeles police had produced a narcotics surveillance videotape showing that the drug lord had been doing a deal in L.A. at the time Al was murdered. In addition, the addict was no longer missing. She had surfaced, alive and well, in San Diego.

When the object of Ty's attention walked out of the bait and tackle shop and vanished around the corner of the building, he didn't have time to tell Ruby to call Biff and have him check out Rianna's safety. All he could do was hang up and go after his quarry as fast as he could without being conspicuous.

When he did catch up, he risked getting closer than he knew was wise. He wanted a better look at what was now protruding out of the rolled-up towel the man still held. It looked too much like a silencer on a gun.

Ty got close enough to feel the hair rise on his scalp; the protruding shape was indeed a silencer. He fell back and cautioned himself to stay calm as he trailed the man to the same public parking lot where he had left his own car that morning. There, a hundred yards from Ty's rented white compact, the man unlocked a too-familiar beige sedan and got in.

Once in his own car, Ty took off his watch cap and wheeled out of the lot several car lengths behind the sedan. He white-knuckled the steering wheel when the sedan headed south from Monterey to Carmel. *Never assume anything.* He gritted his teeth and hammered that reminder home. *Don't assume he's after Rianna. Don't assume he's not. Don't lose sight of him for even one second, you miserable excuse for a bodyguard!*

AT THAT SAME MOMENT in Carmel, Rianna was answering Gordo's knock on the door and inviting him in. After two days of grieving in total seclusion, she had finally cleaned herself up and plugged her phone back into the jack. The first person she'd called had been Gordo. He was more than happy to bring Squeeze-Play over, at Rianna's request, to pose in the flesh.

"You look like the aftermath of a funeral," he scolded after he'd let Squeeze out of her burlap carrying bag in the studio. "Why don't you just go for it, Uncle Nate be damned? Hell, *I'll* give you away at your wedding if he refuses."

"He's already made his position perfectly clear, Gordo."

"That doesn't mean you have to respect it more than you respect yourself and Ty. You're a grown woman with one life to live, for Pete's sake. Why live it without the man you love?"

Rianna shook her head. "I got over being jilted in front of the whole world. I'll get over this, too, in time."

"Speaking of time..." Gordo sighed, checking his watch. "I'm late for lunch with Chloe." He looked at Squeeze, who was taking possession of a square of sunlight on the studio floor. "Talk some sense into her while you're here," he instructed the python. "I'll be back to pick you up after lunch."

EN ROUTE to Carmel, Ty cursed the huge moving van that made it difficult to trail the beige sedan. By the time a space in oncoming traffic allowed him to pass the van, the sedan was out of sight. Finally reaching the Carmel exit, he sped into town, careening around corners with a screech of tires, zooming as fast as the white compact would carry him to Rianna's cottage.

When a police siren sounded behind him, he ignored it and prayed that it was just Biff Gallagher giving chase.

RIANNA CONCENTRATED on painting Squeeze-Play sunning herself. The phone rang. When she answered it, the caller hung up without a word. Wrong number, she told herself and returned to her canvas.

Minutes later, a knock sounded on her door. She checked the studio clock, thinking that Gordo had certainly made his lunch with Chloe the shortest meal in history.

"You'll just have to finish up at a suntan salon later," she told Squeeze and draped the pliant, sun-warmed snake around and over her shoulders like an exotic, wraparound scarf, before going to let Gordo in. She opened the door without checking the peephole.

When she saw the man in the Giants baseball cap standing two feet away, pointing the end of a rolled-up beach towel at her, Rianna froze. She was looking at the barrel of a gun.

This man had come to kill her—just as he'd killed Al. A single shot and she'd be dead.

The gunman, somewhat to her surprise, wore an expression of pure horror. Suddenly she recognized why. Squeeze-Play! He was frozen to the spot when

Squeeze snaked her head out to taste his nose with her long, forked tongue.

Tires screeched to a stop at the curb, and Rianna heard the wail of an approaching siren.

"Rianna!"

Ty leaped toward the gunman in a flying tackle. Before Ty could connect, the gunman toppled backward, apparently trying to escape Squeeze's flicking tongue. As he fell, he swung the gun-filled towel in a wild arc and caught Ty square on the side of the head.

Ty hit the ground with a thud. The gunman fell on top of him. Rianna screamed and lurched forward. Scrambling to his feet, the man dropped the towel, tore his terror-stricken eyes from Squeeze-Play's tongue and escaped through the gate.

Squeeze still draped around her shoulders, Rianna bent to turn Ty over and cradle him in her arms. His eyes were still closed and he wore at least two days' growth of stubble. She stared into his face, fearing the worst.

Dreading that Ty was dying or dead, Rianna felt as if her own life were draining from her. In the past two days she had envisioned an existence without him, but never in such final, unbearable terms.

She clutched him, desperately patting his clammy cheeks, whispered his name and murmured, "Nothing is worth losing you. Yes, my love, I'll defy Father and marry you. I love you, Tyler Toranaga, more than anything in the world."

Right then he moaned and opened his eyes.

"Rainbow?" he breathed.

"Yes. I'm here. Oh, Ty, I—"

She was cut off by the sound of Biff Gallagher's voice beyond the gate. "Halt! Police!" he shouted over a loudspeaker. The command was followed by more screeching of tires, then another order. Rianna saw a blur of beige speed by, then a police car in hot pursuit, its red lights flashing and siren screaming.

Ty struggled to a sitting position, one hand to his head. "What scrambled my brains?"

"That," Rianna said, pointing at the gun lying in the grass beyond the towel, which had unrolled when it went flying.

"Where is he?"

"Biff's pursuing him in the squad car."

Ty rubbed his hands over his eyes, then recoiled; he focused on the python framing Rianna's shoulders. "What in God's name is that?"

Rianna's eyes filled with tears. "The snake who helped you save my life."

"How?"

"Never mind how." Her tears spilled over. "Are you all right, Ty?" she asked, stroking his face.

"Yeah." He fingered an egg-sized lump above his ear and struggled to his feet, bringing her up with him. "Are you? Did he hurt you? Did he—?"

"He never said a word or laid a finger on me," Rianna soothed, moving into his arms as far as she could without crushing Squeeze-Play. "You got here just in time. Where did you come from? How did you know?"

Ten-foot python and all, Ty gathered Rianna close and treasured her. "It's a long story," he said with a sigh, before his lips swooped down to capture hers. "God, I'm so glad you're alive . . . so glad you're alive. . . ."

TWO HOURS LATER, Rianna, Ty and Gordo listened to Biff's account of his chase. Biff had apprehended the gunman a short distance away. Al's files and film had been found in the sedan's trunk. In addition to the gunman, Crayton Thorn and his yacht crew were being held for questioning. A ballistics study was underway to determine if the gun was the same one that had ended Al's life.

"I'll keep your name from leaking out until you get your phone number changed," Biff promised Rianna. "But once word gets out that you've been a murder target, it'll be a news-media field day."

"This time I don't mind," Rianna replied. "If my involvement increases public awareness that endangered animals need more protection, it'll be worth it."

Gordo rolled his eyes. "I'd better change my phone number, too. The last time you made headlines, I had as many reporters calling day and night as you did."

Biff winked at Ty. "They'll be juicy headlines, good buddy. Heiress Saved by Private Eye in Nick of Time. Your business will double overnight."

"What's going to double first is this ostrich egg up the side of my head," Ty retorted, holding an ice pack to the swelling.

"Well, Tyler T," said Biff with a nod to Rianna as he rose to leave, "you got yourself one swell nurse to ease the pain."

Gordo rose with him and hefted the burlap bag that housed Squeeze-Play. "We'll be off, too. By the way, Biff, could you keep Squeeze's name out of this if it ever comes up? Just as a favor to me, the innocent bystander?"

Biff obligingly raised his eyebrows in mock ignorance. "A ten-foot python, you say? *What* ten-foot python?"

Saying goodbye to Biff and Gordo, Rianna turned to Ty. "I'd better call the phone company right away."

"Unplug the phone when you get through."

"Why?"

"Because we have some serious talking to do—after a serious reunion. Don't we?"

"Yes," she said, heading for the phone. "I'll call right now."

Ty drew her back for a clinging kiss. "The reunion takes place in your bed when you're through," he murmured. "I'll be there, waiting."

And when she finished her call and stepped into her bedroom he *was* there. Rakish and still unshaven, with only a towel around his hips, he sprawled on top of the comforter and beckoned her to bed.

"The last two days have felt like two years," he said when she sank into his embrace.

"It's felt like two centuries to me," she whispered, gliding her palms over his chest. "All I've thought about is you."

He traced the rainbow earrings she wore with a fingertip, then the dark circles under her lovely eyes. "How long since you've had a wink of sleep?"

"I can't sleep without you here, Ty. I need you so badly it scares me."

"Tell me what you need."

"You . . . your love. Make love with me, Ty."

"I will, Rainbow. There aren't going to be any more 'last times' for us."

He pressed her onto her back, then straddled her body and stripped her. When she was naked, he knelt, knees hugging her hips, and unwrapped the towel.

"I love you," he murmured, drawing up her hands to his erection.

Rianna curled her fingers around him and slid them back and forth. It thrilled her when he boldly offered himself to her like that and he knew it. It thrilled him, too, to watch her hands caress him. Under the arch of his thighs, her hips undulated in anticipation.

"Soon," he whispered, bending gently to suck her lips and tongue into his mouth, then her nipples and the soft undercurves of her breasts. "Soon, Rainbow . . ."

"Now, Ty," she whispered back, urging his mouth to return to hers and taking possession of his sleek, probing tongue.

He settled his hips between her thighs and let her guide him to her—there he would pour into her all the passion and love he possessed. All of his love he gave her. All of hers he took.

"WILL YOU marry me this time, Rianna Whitney Breece?" he solemnly asked afterward.

"Yes, Ty," she said. "I'll marry you on one condition."

"Name it."

"Forgive my father for the sins of the past. Offer to make peace with him. If he won't accept you after you offer your hand in peace and forgiveness, I'll marry you and we'll live happily ever after without his blessing."

Ty was silent for a long time before he inquired, "Do you know what you're asking?"

"Ty, I know I'm asking a lot. You're a proud man. So is Father. Your family has been hurt. So has his. What I ask is for you to be a bigger man than he is. Shame him into facing what a stubborn, bigoted old man he is. I intend to ask him the same thing I'm asking of you, though I doubt he'll do it. Will you?"

"For us, Rainbow," he decided after a long silence. "For our future, for our children to come, I'm willing to shake hands with him and bury the past."

She could barely speak through her tears of love and gratitude. "I'll call him in the morning and tell him we need to talk."

"Good." He wiped the tears from her eyes. "When shall we get married?"

"Late June. After Chloe and Gordo get back from their honeymoon," she suggested, snuggling against him under the downy comforter. "Or is that too soon?"

Ty gave her a look of mock disappointment. "Tomorrow wouldn't be soon enough for me."

"Afraid you'll lose your nerve if it takes longer?" she teased as she toyed with the silky triangle of black hair on his chest.

"No way I'm going to lose my nerve."

"Why the rush, then?"

"I want you all mine, with my ring on your finger for as long as we both shall live."

"I'm already yours, Ty. So is everything I have."

"Anything with a dollar sign in front of I intend to sign away my right to," he told her in a firm tone that brooked no argument. "We'll live on my income from my agency and yours from your painting or nothing at all."

Rianna sighed her acceptance of that. "How many children shall we have?"

"I don't know. Two? Three? What do you feel up to?"

"Three at the moment. I'm suddenly struck with a severe case of baby lust."

Ty pressed her head more securely into the nook of his shoulder and closed his eyes. He touched her breasts with reverence, imagining them rich with mother's milk. He palmed her flat belly, imagining it round and ripe with the fruit of their love. He imagined himself holding their firstborn to his heart.

He threaded his fingers through the soft curls between her thighs. "Morning and night I'll be after you."

"Don't forget noon," she murmured. "You can always come home for lunch."

"Mmm. Maybe I'll just work out of the house so I don't miss a single opportunity."

"Like the one you're not missing now?"

Ty chuckled. "It's been two days. A man can bottle up a lot of energy in forty-eight hours."

"Silly me to think we'd be able to nap anytime soon." Rianna shifted and abandoned herself to the ever-deeper intimacies his fingers were seeking.

His whisper against her throat was a velvet huskiness. "Would you rather nap?"

"Not now. Later."

"Much later." His breathing came faster as she began to move and moan under the masterstroke of his caress. "In the meantime, tell me you love me."

"I love you."

"Tell me you have to have me."

"I *have* to have you."

"Tell me again that you'll marry me. I still can't believe it."

"I'll marry you."

"A small wedding."

"Where for our honeymoon?"

"Wherever there are more rainbows than anywhere else on earth."

"The Hawaiian Islands win, palms down."

"I love you, Rainbow."

11

IT WAS SUNSET when Ty and Rianna woke in each other's arms.

"I'm starved."

Rianna yawned. "For what?"

"Food, woman, food. The third basic human need after sex and sleep."

"I'm not sure I can even walk, much less throw together an early dinner." Gingerly she stretched her legs and winced.

"Mmm." He grinned sympathetically. "You recover. I'll cook."

He headed into the bathroom, leaving her to marvel in solitude. How much could happen in the space of a day! How had it evolved from tears in the morning to hearing her future husband in the bathroom washing up before dinner? Would wonders never cease?

If only her father could be as loving and willing as Ty to put the past behind him. But Nathan Breece was Nathan Breece. As indomitable as his father before him, he would cast a shadow upon her future with Ty. Even now, on the happiest day of her life, her joy was dimmed by thoughts of Nathan and of the rejection to come.

Tomorrow was soon enough to contemplate it. Tomorrow she would call him, plead with him to bury the past and bless her impending marriage with his approval. If he wouldn't budge on the phone, she'd invite him over to discuss the matter. She had already decided not to tell him that Ty would be present. *That* he could find out for himself after he arrived.

Hearing the rattling of pans, she eased out of bed and claimed the bathroom. After taking a quick shower and dressing in drawstring pants and a rainbow plaid blouse, she joined Ty in the kitchen where dinner was in progress.

"'Pasghetti' tonight," he proclaimed, pressing her onto a counter stool and pouring her a glass of Chianti. "A one-man show. I cook. You watch."

"Can't I at least make the salad?"

"Nope. It's waiting in the fridge, already made. Table's set as you can see. Kick back with your wine."

She obeyed and sat back to watch her bare-chested lover in jeans toss a handful of pasta into a large pot of boiling water. He gave it a stir with a long-handled fork, then lifted the lid on the spaghetti sauce that was simmering in a saucepan.

"Your recipe or mine?" she inquired, sniffing the herb-fragrant air.

"Yours." Ty tossed a telltale empty Ragu jar into the wastebasket under the sink. "Mine takes hours of slaving over a hot stove."

"I'll bet."

"You'll see after we're married. I make a mean Texas chili, too."

"Lucky, lucky me." Rianna smacked her lips. "A man who can cook and the love of my life. What did I do to get so lucky in love?"

Ty clasped her around the hips. "Some women just live right, my rainbow, my love."

"So do some men, it seems." She pressed a kiss into the curve of his neck and breathed in his scent. "Will we ever stop craving each other like this, do you think?"

A heavy knock on the front door sounded before he could open his mouth to reply. Ty lifted one eyebrow. "Who do you know who drops in without calling first?"

"No one."

The knock came again, louder and longer this time.

"It's probably a Girl Scout selling cookies," Ty suggested hopefully.

"Or a reporter bent on a scoop," added Rianna with a grimace.

"I'll get it." Ty slid Rianna back onto the stool, looked down at himself, then back up at her. "Hmm. Maybe I won't. You get it."

Rianna opened the door. "Father! What are you doing here?"

"Making sure you're still alive," Nathan Breece growled. "Why haven't you answered your phone for two days?"

"I—"

"An hour ago I called and got a recording. 'This number is no longer in service.' What's going on?"

"Er—" She cast an anxious glance in the direction of the kitchen, but not a sound could be heard.

"Do I have to stand out here all night?"

Rianna gulped. "Uh. No. Come in." She motioned him in and closed the door.

"Why you live in this pile of boards instead of a normal house, I'll never know," her father said, as he always did, looking around with his customary dismay before he took a seat on the sofa. He brushed a speck off the black dinner jacket he wore and fixed his attention on Rianna. "You're looking well for a woman whose heart was broken two days ago."

"Thank you." She licked her lips with a nervous gesture. "I'm feeling better."

"Well enough to mix me a dry martini before I move on to Mame's for dinner?"

"Sure. I still have the gin you gave me last Christmas."

She scooted into the silent kitchen where Ty was seated on the stool she had vacated—still bare to the waist as she had left him—screwing the top off her bottle of gin.

How he had gotten the gin, a pitcher, a bottle of vermouth and two martini glasses out of the cupboards without making a sound, she couldn't imagine.

He handed her the gin bottle and whispered, "I heard everything. Pour a double for me, too. I'll need it when I face him."

"Face him!" Rianna hissed, fishing ice out of the freezer and putting it into the pitcher before pouring gin over it with a trembling hand. "You can't face him looking like that."

Ty passed a hand over his bare chest. "I don't have much choice. Now's as good a time as any."

"No, it isn't. I haven't talked to him yet." She dashed vermouth into the pitcher.

Ty rose from the stool, took the pitcher from her and stirred it, then filled both martini glasses to the brim. "I'll talk to him," he whispered, lifting a glass in each hand. "Bring your wine. We'll try a three-way toast first and see how it goes."

"Ty, please. Not now."

"It's now or never, Rainbow."

He was steps ahead of her before she rushed after him.

"I hope this is dry enough for you, Mr. Breece," he said, walking straight toward Rianna's father and setting the drink upon the cocktail table in front of him.

"What the—!?" Nathan Breece looked up from his magazine and stared at Ty.

"Father—"

"Sorry we're out of olives," Ty continued smoothly. "We weren't expecting you."

"Expecting me!" the older man sputtered. He glared at Ty, then turned to Rianna. "I thought he was ancient history."

"He was, Father, until today."

She watched Ty extend his hand, heard him say, "I'm Tyler Toranaga. It's a pleasure to finally meet you, sir."

"It's no pleasure to meet *you*, Toranaga," Nathan Breece thundered, ignoring the extended hand. "What are you doing half-naked in my daughter's house?"

"He's having dinner with me."

"I can defend myself, Rianna," Ty said in a low voice.

She glanced sideways at him. "This is my fight, Ty."

He clipped an arm around her shoulders. "It's *our* fight from now on." Looking from Rianna to her father, he said, "We were hoping to talk with you tomorrow, sir, but now that you're here, please hear us out."

Rianna nodded. "Sit down, Father. Please."

"No, thank you. I'll hear you both out standing up."

"Very well, then," said Rianna. "Ty and I plan to be married in late June."

Her father sat down hard. "Married."

"Yes, sir." Ty gritted his teeth.

"Married!" Nathan repeated, louder than before. "I'd die rather than see you marry this . . ."

"I'm going to marry him. Period."

"You won't if I refuse to give you away at your wedding."

"That won't change my mind, Father. I owe my life to him."

"You owe nothing. Not a cent of your fortune, you hear?"

"I'll sign any financial agreement you care to draw up, sir."

"Damn it, Toranaga. Stop addressing me as if either of us had a shred of respect for each other."

Ty drew a deep, calming breath. "I respect you enough as my future father-in-law to let the past rest in peace. Sir."

The older man blinked. "You what?"

"I'm willing to let bygones be bygones."

"What do your parents have to say about this?"

"I don't know. I haven't told them yet. But I can tell you one thing, Mr. Breece. They *will* be at my wedding, even if only to save face. If Rianna had saved my life as I saved hers, they'd even make themselves smile."

"What in the hell do you mean, 'saved hers'?" Nathan Breece barked.

"Ty means you'd be arranging the details of my funeral right now had it not been for him." Rianna held up her thumb and forefinger a fraction of an inch apart.

"I came this close to getting shot on my doorstep by a hired gunman."

Her father paled. "Shot! What hired gunman?"

"A man hired by an exotic-animal smuggler who didn't want me identifying him in court."

"What court? Where?"

"It's a long story," Ty put in. "It'll be all over the news tomorrow. Long story short, I got here just in time to foil an attempt on Rianna's life."

Nathan Breece sat back and just looked at them standing there together. "*You* saved my only daughter's life? When?"

"Earlier today."

"And it's going to hit the news wires tomorrow?"

Ty nodded. "If it hasn't already."

Rianna's father looked from her to Ty and shook his head. "*You* saved her life."

"I did, sir."

"Single-handedly?"

"Well, I—" Ty caught Rianna's warning look and mentally apologized to Squeeze-Play. "I did everything I could," he hedged.

"She wouldn't be alive now if it hadn't been for you."

"Probably not, sir."

For several long moments Nathan Breece was silent, staring at the martini in front of him.

Rianna regarded him with growing alarm as he heaved a shuddering sigh. She took a step toward him. "Father, are you all right?"

"Leave me be. I never thought I'd see the day I'd ever be grateful to a . . . a . . ."

"Japanese-American?" Ty supplied with a wry smile.

Rianna's father nodded and hung his head. Slowly, as if it were agony to make so gentlemanly a gesture, he extended his hand to Ty. "She's all I have. It appears I owe you more than money can buy."

"Your blessing is all we ask," said Ty, clasping his future father-in-law's hand and shaking it firmly.

"She's too good for you," Nathan Breece muttered.

"Yes, sir. Parents being parents, mine will say the same about me to Rianna when they give us *their* blessing."

Rianna caught her breath as light from the setting sun streamed through the stained glass window on the west wall. Tears gathered in her eyes at the sight of radiant, rainbow hues bathing the clasped hands of the two men she loved most in the world.

She touched her hand to theirs and knew with no doubt that wishes on rainbows *are* wishes come true.

GREAT NEWS...

HARLEQUIN UNVEILS NEW SHIPPING PLANS

For the convenience of customers, Harlequin has announced that Harlequin romances will now be available in stores at these convenient times each month*:

Harlequin Presents, American Romance, Historical, Intrigue:

May titles: April 10
June titles: May 8
July titles: June 5
August titles: July 10

Harlequin Romance, Superromance, Temptation, Regency Romance:

May titles: April 24
June titles: May 22
July titles: June 19
August titles: July 24

We hope this new schedule is convenient for you.

With only two trips each month to your local bookseller, you'll never miss any of your favorite authors!

*Please note: There may be slight variations in on-sale dates in your area due to differences in shipping and handling.

HDATES-RR

*Applicable to U.S. only.